PRAISE FOR *CHASER*

"For those who don't know Miasha (*Never Enough*), it's time to get on board with this outstanding writer. Her bold strokes balance the violence of drug dealing with fellas making quick cash any way possible. What makes her latest soar is the spot-on slang and trash-talking dialogue, which is both joking and profane. Plus, tension crackles off her pages. Street lit fans will be thrusting this title into their friends' hands, demanding that they read it. Buy multiple copies."

— *Library Journal*

"*Chaser* is a fast-paced street romantic suspense starring a young woman who learns the hard way what matters in life. Fans who relish a different kind of contemporary romance will want to read Leah's tale of struggling to survive the mean streets of Philadelphia."

— **Harriet Klausner**

"Miasha introduces us to *Chaser*, another fast-paced page-turner in her heavy-hitting arsenal of novels. Though filled with enough cash, imported cars, and designer labels to entice the most status-conscious reader, Miasha's *Chaser* is a reminder that every choice has a consequence. True Miasha fans will certainly enjoy this book, while new readers will appreciate the thought-provoking story line that's cleverly wrapped up in a not-so-ordinary package.

— **Sistah Confessions Book Club (Baltimore, MD)**

PRAISE FOR *MOMMY'S ANGEL*

"Miasha keeps things moving at a fast clip, but the basic empathy and understanding that pervade are the story's real appeal. [She] never loses sight of the basic humanity of all the lost souls that surround Angel."

— *Publishers Weekly*

"In the midst of all the same voices in literature, Miasha brings authenticity to the pages of this novel. She's the crème de la crème—enjoy!"

—Vickie Stringer, *Essence* bestselling author of
Let That Be the Reason

"*Mommy's Angel* highlights some of the harsh realities that many of our society's poor and forgotten children face in life . . . Earthy, realistic, and full of unpredictable twists and turns, Miasha has written a novel that is sure to please."

—Rawsistaz.com

"*Mommy's Angel* is a fast-paced, well-written, realistic view of what addiction does to our communities. It sheds a bright light on how the addict's hurt, pain, and trouble are recycled onto the people closest to them."

—Danielle Santiago, author of *Grindin'* and *Essence* #1
bestseller *Little Ghetto Girl*

"A poignant tale of innocence lost in Brooklyn."

—K'wan, author of *Gangsta, Street Dreams, Eve,* and *Hood Rat*

PRAISE FOR *DIARY OF A MISTRESS*

"Miasha cleverly builds up the suspense and throws in several unexpected twists. Her latest release is filled with intrigue and will keep you turning the pages. *Diary of Mistress* will make you think twice about who you trust."

—Sheila M. Goss, e-Spire Entertainment editor and author of
My Invisible Husband

"Miasha has done it again. *Diary of a Mistress* is a sizzling novel full of unexpected twists and guaranteed to leave readers in shock, and gasping for air, as they excitedly turn each page."

—Karen E. Quinones Miller, author of *Satin Doll, I'm Telling,*
and *Satin Nights*

"*Diary of a Mistress* is an intense, captivating, and twisted love triangle. Miasha allows the usually silent mistress to raise her voice through the pages of her diary."

—Daaimah S. Poole, author of
Ex-Girl to the Next Girl, *What's Real*, and *Got a Man*

"Only Miasha can make it hard to choose between wanting to be the mistress or the wife."

—Brenda L. Thomas, author of *Threesome*, *Fourplay*, and
The Velvet Rope

PRAISE FOR *SECRET SOCIETY*

"Scandalous and engrossing, this debut from Miasha . . . shows her to be a writer to watch."

—*Publishers Weekly*

"A sizzling and steamy novel . . . The storyline will hold readers' attention and entertain them in the process."

—*Booking Matters*

"Miasha enters the arena of urban literature full-throttle and ready to swing . . . surely to become one the most talked-about novels of 2006."

—Mahogany Book Club (Albany NY)

"Miasha cooks up a delicious drama with all the ingredients of a bestseller— seduction, vindication, and lots of scandal."

—Brenda L. Thomas, author of *Threesome*, *Fourplay*, and
The Velvet Rope

"Miasha tells it like it is. Her writing style is gritty and gripping, and will keep you reading and wanting more."

—Karen E. Quinones Miller, author of *Ida B*

Also by Miasha

Chaser
Never Enough
Sistah for Sale
Mommy's Angel
Diary of a Mistress
Secret Society

'Til Death

Miasha

A Touchstone Book
Published by Simon & Schuster
New York   London   Toronto   Sydney

Touchstone
A Division of Simon & Schuster, Inc.
1230 Avenue of the Americas
New York, NY 10020

First Touchstone trade paperback edition September 2010

TOUCHSTONE and colophon are registered trademarks of
Simon & Schuster, Inc.

For information about special discounts for bulk purchases,
please contact Simon & Schuster Special Sales at 1-866-506-1949
or business@simonandschuster.com.

The Simon & Schuster Speakers Bureau can bring authors
to your live event. For more information or to book an event
contact the Simon & Schuster Speakers Bureau at 1-866-248-3049
or visit our website at www.simonspeakers.com.

Manufactured in the United States of America

10   9   8   7   6   5   4   3   2   1

Library of Congress Cataloging-in-Publication Data
Miasha, 1981–
    'Til death / Miasha. — 1st Touchstone trade paperback ed.
        p.   cm.
    "A Touchstone book."
    1. African American women — Fiction. I. Title.
    PS3613.I18T55 2010
    813'.6–dc22   2010025089

ISBN 978-1-4165-8988-4
ISBN 978-1-4165-9752-0 (ebook)

I dedicate this one to all my fans
who've been reading my books since day one.
I put this one together especially for you!

"What about the so-called pact we had? Huh? What happened to that? 'Til death, remember?" I screamed at Si-Si

"*This is death!*" she yelled back, then she paused. She looked around as if she was trying to see whether our outbursts were bringing any unwanted attention our way. Then she took a second to gather her composure. "Death to Sienna, death to Si-Si, death to Vida," she said in a much lower tone.

"What are you talkin' about, Si-Si?" I asked, too frustrated and too high to figure out any riddles.

"The life we were living is over, Celess. It's a wrap. Give it up. Turn yourself in. The streets are not safe for you."

"And they're safe for you?" I asked. "What, you want me to cover my whole body? Will that make me safe? 'Cause if that's what you want, I'll do it. But I'm not turning myself in!" I said. "Not unless you are!" I added.

"Well, that's your choice." She gave no argument. "Whatever you decide to do, that's on you."

"Okay, cool. Now that we have that understanding, what

are you going to do? I say we hook up with some of these rich-ass oil niggas and build us an empire off they dime." I wanted bad to get back the life Si-Si and I had when it was good.

"I'm done with all that, Celess." Si-Si shook her head. "Last night," she began slowly and steadily, as if the words that were about to come off her tongue were fragile, "Amir took me to take my *shahada*. Then this morning we went . . . and got married."

I was in total and utter shock, almost speechless, but I was able to yell out, "*What?*"

Si-Si looked around again. Then she explained, "Celess, I don't wanna end up like my mom." Tears began to escape her light-brown eyes, which was all I could see of her. "Or like all the other women I've known throughout my life. I *want* to grow old someday. I wanna settle down and have children, watch them grow and play and laugh and learn, and just witness a normal existence before I leave this earth. And I don't see that happening if I continue on this path. All the sex and the drugs, the alcohol and the partying, it's all a waste," she said, shaking her head. "Wasted energy, wasted money, wasted time. I mean, we had our fun, yes, I'll admit that. But realistically," she paused, looked down and back up, then she continued, "how long will it last?" Si-Si wiped her eyes and took a breath. She shrugged her shoulders, and with the most sincere look in her eyes, she said, "I want a *real* life, Celess, not just a fast one."

Too bad I wasn't buying it. I mean, not only was it sudden and random, like many decisions Si-Si made, but I was high, and she was blowin' it. I rolled my eyes and folded my arms, resting them across my stomach. I was so ready to dismiss all that Si-Si was saying. I mean, we had been through so much shit together, and for her to just turn her back on me for some nigga she practically just met didn't make any sense to me. I was sure she was just talking out her ass. Amir got in her ear a little bit, broke her off some good dick, and flashed his wealth before her—and she was ready to submit. I was sure she just needed a wake-up call.

"We're still young, Si-Si! You actin' like we 'bout to croak! We have our whole lives to change," I reminded her, thinking about the ten years, minimum, that we had left to play.

Si-Si didn't say anything. She just looked around, her eyes bouncing from one golden dome to the next. I thought I had her, and I started to seal the deal with a plan for us both to switch out of the fast lane in 2014. I figured we could agree to at least five more years of making money and moves. But right before I had the chance to propose we make a deal, she said something that sent chills down my spine.

"Celess, you need to get out of the game while you still *have* your life to change."

I unfolded my arms and brought my hands to my face, holding them over my eyes for a second. The last time I heard someone say something like that to me, I didn't take heed. And not only did I come close to death, but I also lost the dearest person to me.

I had mixed emotions. I didn't know what to say or do, but right then on that rooftop in Dubai, my life with Si-Si up until that moment flashed before my eyes like scenes from an action movie. Taking me back to the beginning, fifteen months ago, when she and I first stepped off the plane in Rome.

October 2007

"I got a million text messages," Si-Si said as soon as her phone booted up.

"You too?" I asked, glancing down at my phone as I briskly walked beside her through the Leonardo da Vinci Airport headed toward baggage claim. It was a quarter after four. We had been in the air for close to sixteen hours since we departed Los Angeles the day before. The Rome airport was extra crowded for some reason. I mean, yes, it was a Friday, and I'm sure that had a lot to do with there being lots of travelers, but goodness, there had to be another reason for the massive number of people entering Rome on that day.

"David is worried sick," Si-Si said of the famous Hollywood actor she had fallen in love with several months back. "He's like, 'Call me, please. They're saying you're either dead or running from the law . . .'" She whispered one of the many messages she had on her phone.

I looked at her as she scrolled her Dash with the same pity in my eyes that she had in her voice, and I huffed. I knew it had to be hard on her, abruptly leaving David and then not being able to let him know she was safe.

"I wish I could call him of all people," she continued. "Just to tell him I'm okay."

Like I figured, I thought. I didn't say anything, but it was a good thing that Si-Si read my silence correctly and didn't make the call.

"I just think we need to get somewhere safe before we decide what we're goin' to do and who we're goin' to call."

Si-Si nodded in agreement. "You're right," she said. "We gotta be smart."

"Everything we do and say gotta be thought out," I added. I looked at Si-Si for her response, and she nodded again, although she didn't seem to be paying me much attention anymore. Instead, she was focused on the crowd of people standing before us holding signs up for whomever they were there to pick up.

"Where is Andrew?" she mumbled, her eyes squinting.

"Call him," I said.

"Damn it!" she exclaimed. "I was supposed to call him as soon as we landed so he could meet us at baggage claim." She threw one hand on her forehead, while the other palmed her phone. Then she mumbled, "All those texts threw me off. And that message from David . . ."

Si-Si was shaken up, I could tell. I'd never seen her so disoriented before. I decided to take charge: It was clear to me that she was overwhelmed.

"Here, you sit down and call Andrew." I led her to a bench. "I'll go get your bags."

Si-Si did as I told her, and she took a seat. Even sitting, she couldn't keep still. Her legs were trembling. I watched her for a moment before walking over to the luggage carousel, then turned to check on her often. I felt the need to keep a close eye on her. She seemed so unstable. I imagined she was still shook up about having killed that guy back home. And how could I blame her?

No sooner did the carousel begin dishing out the bags, than Si-Si's luggage fell onto the belt. The beauty of first class, I thought. I reached out to grab them as they got near, but a gentleman on his cell phone intervened.

"Excuse me, sir," I said as I sized him up. He was a medium-height white guy with some edge and even a little bit of swagger. He had on a fresh pair of blue, green, and white Dsquared^2 sneakers, a matching V-neck long-sleeve tee, and a pair of True Religion jeans. His dark curly hair peeked through a navy True Religion trucker hat.

"Are you with Sienna?" he asked, ending his call and putting his cell in his jeans pocket.

"Sienna?" I questioned, confused by his approach and briefly mesmerized by his sexiness. Then a lightbulb went off in my head, and I said, "Oh, yes, Si-Si. You must be Andrew."

"Yes," he said, nodding. "And you are the friend she just told me about."

"Celess." I shook the hand he freed up for our formal introduction, now wondering why Si-Si had just told him about me.

"Yes, Celess. I'm sorry," he said. "Si-Si didn't mention to me that she was bringing someone until now. But it's certainly nice to meet you."

"Oh." I paused. "Well, I hope it's not a problem."

"No, not at all. I'm assuming you have bags as well?"

I shook my head. "Actually, no . . . I . . . They lost my luggage." I lied real quick. I sure wasn't about to tell him that I had no time to bring my luggage because I was running for my life.

"Oh, good, because I was going to have to ask you to leave yours behind too. They won't fit in my car, so you two will just have to get new things."

"Oh . . . okay," I said, impressed.

"So take me to Sienna?" he said anxiously. "I'm dying to see that girl."

"She's right over here," I said, as I led him away from the carousel and over toward where Si-Si was sitting. "We thought we'd be waiting a little while for you to get here, seeing as how Si-Si was supposed to call you as soon as we touched down."

"Oh, well, she called when you guys boarded and told me everything was on time so . . . I actually got here earlier than I'd planned, and I just parked. Figured I'd wait for her at baggage claim," he explained, briskly walking one step behind me.

"Si-Si!" I called out.

She looked up in my direction. Her eyes were locked on me until I got closer to her. They then drifted past me and landed on Andrew.

"Andrew!" she squealed as she stood up to hug him.

He chuckled as he squeezed her in his arms. "Well looky, here," Andrew said, standing back to look Si-Si over. "Where have you been, Sienna? What have you been doing?"

Si-Si looked at him, almost staring. Her eyes were watery. She shrugged her shoulders and said, "Just . . . living." Then she cracked a huge smile as if to keep from crying.

Andrew smiled as well. "Yeah? Well, I hope living good."

"As good as life gets," she replied.

"Good," he said. "What brings you to my side of the world? It's been so many years. I thought you forgot about me." Andrew stood stiffly, as if paralyzed by Si-Si's presence.

"I could never forget you, Andrew," Si-Si said. "Just been trying out independence, that's all."

"How you like it?"

"It's good. It's good. Just can get awfully lonely."

"So you missed me?"

"That's one of the reasons I'm here."

"What would be another?" Andrew asked.

"Just needed a change of scenery. One's own world can get so repetitive. It never hurts to put it on pause and visit someone else's."

Si-Si had a way with words. I swear she had more game than me.

"Well, let's go. I have a lot of things planned for us," Andrew said, finally ending the small talk.

"I hope the first thing involves gettin' a drink. Because I need one," Si-Si said.

"Oh, where I'm taking you, there will be champagne for days, my friend."

"And where might that be?" Si-Si asked.

"To Genoa, the biggest boat show in the world. You came at the perfect time," Andrew told her as he grabbed her hand and started to lead us out of the airport.

"Um, wait a minute, where are my bags?" Si-Si remembered.

He shook his head. "I stopped your friend from getting them," he said. "Whatever's in them won't stand up to what they have at the shops in Via XX Settembre, believe me. Besides, they won't fit in my car. In fact, we're gonna have to squeeze your friend in. I didn't know you weren't coming alone."

"Yeah, that was my fault," Si-Si said. "I had so much going on you wouldn't believe, and I just was so happy to get in touch with you, it completely slipped my mind to tell you I was bringing Celess. I hope that's no problem."

Andrew grinned. "Nothing's a problem when you're with me," he told her. "You know that." He put his arm around her shoulder and guided her outside.

In that moment Si-Si lit up. Her whole energy changed. She went from being frazzled and a bit lost to seeming whole again. I guessed she felt a sense of security with her old friend. And when we got outside to his car, I could see why.

This handsome Italian guy led us to a white Bugatti Veyron with red leather interior and white piping. The only time I had ever seen one was in an issue of the *Robb Report* a while back. The picture did it no justice. It was to die for. If we were going to be stuck on another continent for who knew how long, I was soooo happy and relieved to know that we would be staying with money. Hell, I felt secure too.

Si-Si glanced back at me with a grin on her face. We made eye contact, but that was it. We both remained silent as we lapped it in the passenger seat of the 1.4 million-dollar car.

We pulled up to yet another airport, where a private plane was waiting for us. At first, I figured Andrew had chartered it, but after getting on board and seeing his signature engraved in all of the headrests, I knew he actually owned the aircraft. Impressive. Si-Si called the right one, I thought. My problems back home were fading away faster than I thought they could. And I wondered for a minute whether it was normal for someone to be so obsessed with money and fine things that nothing else in the wide world mattered. But, hell, I never was considered normal in the first place. So why worry about fitting that description now?

"So how long's this flight?" Si-Si asked Andrew as she helped herself to a glass of white wine.

"It's just over two hundred miles. We'll be on the ground in no time."

"Well, good, because I'm *so* over being in the sky right now."

"I bet," Andrew said, taking a seat beside Si-Si.

As soon as he sat down, Si-Si rested her head on his shoulder. I watched the two and admired the Kodak moment. Moreover, I felt happy for Si-Si. I knew she was distraught about having seen her mother murdered and then having pulled the trigger on a man. I could only imagine what emotions she was feeling. I was just glad that she had someone in addition to me to lean on. Especially someone as rich as Andrew.

When we landed in Genoa and got off the plane, Andrew led us to another white Bugatti with red leather interior and white piping. It was exactly like the one we had left in Rome. I did a double take.

Si-Si shot Andrew a look like she was thinking the same thing I was, and Andrew explained himself.

"I like what I like," he said.

Boy, oh boy, I thought, this guy was stuntin' hard, and I couldn't help but be turned on by him. Nevertheless, I maintained my composure. He was Si-Si's friend. Besides, I was sure he had someone he could hook me up with when that time came. And what I was even surer about was the fact that whoever that might be had the same type of money Andrew obviously had. Everybody knows birds of a feather flock together. So I would be patient.

We positioned ourselves in the passenger seat again and were off. I hoped we weren't in for a long ride, because sitting on Si-Si's lap in the two-seater was uncomfortable. The one thing I did enjoy, though, was being able to see the sights. Italy was a beautiful place—refreshing even. I mean, the architecture there made me want to cry. Honestly, I had never seen anything so unique and prestigious. I thought about my best friend, Tina, and the time she'd visited Derek's family in Italy during their monthlong honeymoon, and I remembered her telling me how beautiful this country was. She was so right. Quickly, I changed the subject in my head. It had been years since Tina was killed, but thinking about her was bound to have me break out into tears. And God knows, I didn't want to do that in front of Andrew. He had just met me not even an hour ago, and I didn't want his first impression of me to be that I was this emotional, crazy chick. I turned my attention to the amazingly beautiful vehicle I was in.

After admiring every detail, from the navigation screen in the rearview mirror to the key, which resembled a small pocketknife, I decided to break the silence.

"How much is on the dash?" I asked Andrew.

Without taking his eyes off the spiraling road, he replied, "A little over two fifty."

"Wow," I said.

Quickly glancing at me, he boasted, "And it gets there in less than a minute."

I nodded my head slowly and repeated, "Wow."

"So what does one have to do to get a car like this?"

"Well, place an order."

"And what's that process?"

"Just three hundred and fifty USD," he said nonchalantly.

"Three hundred and fifty thousand dollars is needed just to place the order?" I had to verify.

Andrew nodded. "Pretty much."

Even Si-Si commented on that one. "So while other guys

are buying Bentleys or Ferraris, Andrew here is using that money just to order his car," she said, boosting his already big ego. "Gotta love it," she concluded.

"Got to," I added.

After a quick ten-minute drive from the Genoa airport, we arrived at the Bentley Hotel, a modern, luxurious structure with the perfect name. The valet parking attendant was at our door instantaneously.

"Mr. Coselli." The guy nodded his hello to Andrew.

Andrew put some folded bills in his palm and patted him on the shoulder as he made room for the young man to take his place in the driver's seat.

We went inside the five-star hotel, and the lobby reminded me of one of Vegas's most upscale spots. The Art Deco meets couture décor gave a rich and futuristic feel. We checked into the room Andrew had reserved. Good thing it was a suite, because I had my own room. I could enjoy my privacy, and Si-Si and Andrew could enjoy theirs. I didn't have any bags or anything, so I didn't have much settling in to do. All I did upon entering the luxurious bedroom was come out of my dirty clothes, take a nice long bath, cover up in the complimentary bathrobe, and plop down on the bed. I attempted to watch some TV, but the language barrier and my exhaustion made that impossible. I was asleep in no time.

I awakened to the smell of hot breakfast, despite the fact it was already lunchtime. Indeed, I had slept well into the next day. My body needed the rest. I stretched and got up out of bed. I went to the bathroom, washed my face, and brushed my teeth. Then I went into the living room to see where the aroma of bacon and eggs was coming from.

"Good afternoon," Andrew said as he ate his well-balanced breakfast. He was fully dressed.

"Good afternoon," I said. "I didn't mean to sleep so late. Is Si-Si up and dressed too?"

"No, she's out like a light," he said, focusing on getting a piece of his omelet on his fork. "She didn't sleep well last night. Tossed and turned a lot," he said.

"Oh," I said. "She had trouble sleeping on the plane too."

"Yeah, that's flying commercial for you," he said, then he asked, "You want breakfast? There's plenty in there. I figured I'd order everything on the menu rather than wake you two."

"Thank you," I said. "I'm starving." I moved toward the food display.

Andrew wasn't exaggerating. He really had bought the entire menu. Once again I was impressed. He was continuously outdoing himself. He was his own competition. That's a rich nigga for you, I thought.

"So, Celess, right?" Andrew decided to strike up a conversation.

"Yes."

"You and Sienna were both big actresses in the United States, huh?"

"Well, we were certainly working on it," I said modestly.

"I see. That's interesting. The last time I saw Sienna she was this young, ambitious girl with so much drive and passion. I knew she would go on to do big things."

"Yeah, that's exactly how she was when I met her," I said, recalling the day I had been shopping at the boutique Si-Si worked in and how she had quit on the spot after I told her I could show her how to get money. I smirked at that memory. To this day, I had never met somebody so fearless.

"Well, today is the first day of Salone Nautico Internazionale—"

"The what?" I interrupted Andrew.

"The International Boat Show. It's an annual thing. They showcase some of the biggest and best yachts."

"Oh, right. I remember, yes, of course."

"Yeah. And, uh, I have my eye on something, so I need to be there." He glanced at his watch. "I'm going to leave some money, so when sleeping beauty awakes, you two can have a driver take you to Via XX Settembre to get some clothes and things. It's within meters of here. You could actually walk, but I wouldn't want you to do that. And once you get done, call me and I will meet up with you. Okay?"

I nodded. "Sure. Thanks."

Andrew disappeared in the room he and Si-Si shared for a few minutes, then he reentered the small living room. He was carrying a wad of cash. I thought he was going to peel a few bills from the wad and hand them to me, but he gave me the entire thing.

"Get something nice. I want you two to be the most beautiful girls there. Not that that should be hard. But you know what I mean."

"No worries," I said. "We know how to show up."

Andrew grinned, and I took notice at how clean he looked. He wasn't wearing a hat, and his hair was slicked back, allowing his thick, dark eyebrows to take center stage. He cleaned up well for the boat show, I thought. I watched him gather some of his belongings, which included a sports jacket and a briefcase, and head out the door. "See you later," he said.

As soon as the door slammed behind him, I started counting the money. There were 575 bills altogether. Two hundred of them were 500-euros bills, and the other 375 were 200-euros bills. That equaled 175,000 euros. Now, what the hell was that in USD? I was eager to know. I went in the bedroom where Si-Si was oversleeping.

"Si-Si, wake up already!" I started opening the drapes, figuring the bright sunshine would help. "Si-Si!"

"Huuuh?" Si-Si sighed as she slowly rolled over in the bed.

"Wake up, girl, ya friend left us a mountain of cash to go shopping, and now I can't sit still!"

I sat on the edge of the bed next to Si-Si's head. After rubbing her eyes repeatedly, she sat up.

"What?" she asked. "What are you so hype about?"

I waved the money in her face, and with a Kool-Aid smile, I said, "This."

"Where did you get that from? Where is Andrew?"

"He left to go to that boat show. He said for us to take this and get something to wear for today. He said he want us to be the baddest bitches at the show."

Si-Si shook her head. "He didn't say that."

"Well, not in those exact words, but that's what he meant. Now get up, shower, and let's go do some damage!"

Si-Si didn't budge. Instead, she just shook her head as if to say, Um, um, um.

"What's wrong?" I questioned her lack of enthusiasm.

Then as if she had just snapped out of a daze, she said, "Nothing." And with a more upbeat tone and attitude she said, "Let's go."

It took Si-Si and me only about a half hour to get dressed. All we had to do was shower and throw on the same clothes from the previous day. We both felt dirty and uncomfortable, but it was only for a short period. We called for a car service like Andrew instructed and had the driver take us shopping. It was in the car that Si-Si counted the money for herself. She knew how to convert the currency and everything.

"Two hundred and fifty," she said when she was done.

"You are lying to me!" I couldn't believe that Andrew had given us $250,000 cash money, right off the bat.

"No, I'm not," Si-Si said. "He's megarich, Celess. This to him is nothing."

"What the hell, he print money?"

Si-Si chuckled and said, "Something like that."

I paused and looked up at Si-Si, my eyebrows furrowed. I needed clarification. I mean, I wasn't about to be spending no counterfeit money, especially not while I was already running from the law.

"Not like that," she said, reading my thoughts. "He owns stock in the Federal Reserve," she explained. "Lots of it."

"As much as I love money, I don't know what the Federal Reserve is."

"Put it this way." Si-Si broke it down. "He practically owns the U.S. Mint."

"Shit, girl! Why the hell we ain't been come out here? Are you kiddin' me?"

She smirked and said, "I told you the money over here was much longer."

"Well, I don't know about you, but I ain't never goin' back to the States," I said.

"Never say never," Si-Si quoted.

"You heard me clear, bitch, *never*! Matter fact, how do you say never in Italian?"

We were dropped off in one of the most expensive shopping districts in Genoa. We tipped our driver and hit the pavement, headed to Coin, an internationally known designer department store.

"I want the entire window," I said, peeking at the glamorous wares that draped all the mannequins.

Inside, Si-Si and I went from designer section to designer section, grabbing everything from lingerie and pajamas to shoes and jackets and everything in between, including makeup and perfume. After Coin, it was Strenesse, a haute-couture boutique near the Carlo Felice Theater. Then it was Fedra, a shop that sold high fashion names like Yves Saint Laurent and Sonia Rykiel. We spent about six hours and just over 90,000 euros when it was all said and done. We grabbed a late lunch at Zeffirino, a famous family-owned restaurant that served what had to be the best-tasting ravioli in the world.

Afterward, we hit our driver up to take us back to our hotel, where we showered again and changed into our new clothes. We both opted to wear Emanuel Ungaro. I was in a sleeveless gray minidress with a rock-and-roll-type print splashed with red, black, and silver sequins and crystals. I carried a red leather waist-length motorcycle jacket to shield me from the typical by-the-water breeze. On my feet was a pair of red ankle boots by Dior. Si-Si wore a pair of high-waisted royal blue ski pants with a cream strip going down the side of each leg and a gold zipper from the waist to the hip. Tucked into them was a black bodysuit, which she covered with a cropped-sleeve black blazer. On her hands she wore a pair of cream leather biker gloves. She wore a simple pair of black wedge-heeled pumps, also Ungaro.

Andrew was going to get his wish because we were sure to

be the best-looking girls ever to attend the boat show—in all its fortysomething years.

Once we were ready to go, Si-Si called Andrew to find out where he wanted us to meet him. He told her to have the driver take us to Porto Antico, which turned out to be around the corner. We didn't know where or what that was, but the driver did and that was all that mattered.

We arrived at our destination within minutes. It was a port from which people could take a ferry to Fiera di Genova, the venue for the boat show. We asked Andrew if he wanted us to take the ferry, and he instructed us just to wait at the port. He would meet us there—and that he did, in a sleek, stainless-steel-looking yacht.

At that point I was no longer amazed at Andrew's wealth and how he flaunted it. I stepped onto the powerboat as if it had been my means of transportation for years, with both my head and my nose to the sky. You couldn't tell me anything!

"We're taking a boat to the boat show," Si-Si said, settling into the passenger seat of the Porsche-designed cruiser. "How fitting."

"It's too much road traffic to go by car," Andrew reasoned with a grin on his face.

He knew road traffic had nothing to do with his picking us up in his $300,000 watercraft. I mean, we were only minutes away from the convention center. We could've walked in the time it took him to get to the port. He just wanted to stunt like he'd been doing the entire time. I fucked with it, though.

"You look stunning, by the way," Andrew complimented Si-Si. "You and Celess both."

"Courtesy of my favorite bachelor," Si-Si replied.

I chimed in, "Yes, all thanks to you."

"Anything for this one," Andrew said, nodding toward Si-Si. "She holds a special place in my heart."

Si-Si blushed, and I picked up on a chemistry between the two that I admired. I mean, I could tell Si-Si was holding back, probably because she was still feeling sorrowful about her mom and how we left the States, which I couldn't blame her for. But I did wish she would snap out of it. I didn't want her emotions to consume her. I of all people knew how dangerous that could be. I made a mental note to pull her to the side and talk to her about it as soon as we reached land.

"Can I have a minute with Si-Si, please, Andrew?" I asked as he helped me off the boat and onto the marina slip.

Andrew let go of my hand once I'd planted my feet on sturdy ground. "Sure," he said. "We have a suite right inside here. Just come on in when you're ready."

"Okay." I nodded. "Thanks."

The minute Andrew disappeared, Si-Si turned to me. "What's up?" she asked.

"How are you feeling?" I got to the point.

"Fine," Si-Si said. "Why? What's wrong?"

"Nothing's wrong with me. But you seem to go in and out. And I know we didn't really get to talk about what we were going to do from here, so maybe you still feel a little confused or overwhelmed or whatever. But I just want you to know that I'm here for you if you need to talk, get some things off your chest, or even if you just need to cry. I don't want you to bottle anything up inside. I want you to be all right."

Si-Si didn't say anything at first. She just looked around.

Then after some time she blurted, "Celess, I'm scared. I am so scared."

"I knew it was something," I told her.

"Look," she said, pulling her cell phone from her purse.

I leaned forward to view her screen.

She pulled up a more recent text message from David. It read: *Just need to hear something. Cops found a gun with your prints on it. They're saying you killed a man. What is going on? I'm worried!*

"You text him?" I asked her.

She didn't answer, but the look on her face said yes. "I had to," she confessed. "I had to let him know I was safe, and I needed to know what was being said back home."

"You didn't tell him where we were, did you?"

Si-Si shook her head.

I looked out at the endless ocean. The sun was setting beneath the calm waves. The view was breathtaking. I exhaled and turned my attention back to Si-Si.

"Listen," I told her, "I'm not goin' lie. I've been a little worried myself. I mean, I got messages from Ms. Carol, Sean, and even Michael, all talking about how they seen the murders on the news and how the police were naming us suspects." I confessed about having heard from my shrink and two ex-boyfriends.

Si-Si cut me off. "What are we gonna do, Celess? I mean, should we go back and just turn ourselves in and tell them everything?"

I shook my head. "Hell, no. I'm not tryna go to jail."

"But it was self-defense. I mean, he was going to kill us. He *killed* my mom." Si-Si looked as if she was going to break down.

"That's true but hard to prove. His back was turned when

you shot him. And them twisted laws been done had us both doing time just for protecting our lives. It's too risky."

"Well, what, then? We can't stay out here forever."

"Why can't we?" I asked. "You said it yourself, here we can make ten times the money we made back home. So why not stay out here and do just that? I mean, we clearly see it's possible. Look at us, look where we are, what we have on, what we been riding in. It don't get no better than this."

"I know I said that, but that was before what happened to my mom and before what I did. Now, it's different. I feel so hurt and paranoid, I can't really enjoy all of this. It's like my mind will only let me escape it for a short while. Then it haunts me all over again."

"I understand. I do. But with time it will fade, trust me. But you don't wanna be spending that time in nobody's cell, constantly reminded of the tragedy that put you there. I don't know about you, but I'd much rather be spending that time eating chocolate-covered strawberries and sipping champagne on somebody's yacht. You just need time, that's all. I say we put the whole thing behind us and act like it never happened."

"Are you okay with that, though? I mean, what if they eventually track us down?"

"I say we get rid of our phones. Leave everything that ties us to the past in the past. Leave no traces."

"Are you sure? Because God forbid, if that was to happen, if they do catch up to us, you would be in more trouble then than you are now. I don't want to drag you down with me."

"This is my choice, Si-Si. It ain't like you got me in some third-world country shacked up in a hut. We livin' good, and it ain't even been forty-eight hours yet. Can you imagine what we could be living like with more time to connect and to put some shit together?" I paused briefly. Then I reminded Si-Si, "I told you on the plane after you came clean to me, I'm ridin', and I meant that."

Tears gathered in Si-Si's eyes as she began to take the back of her phone off. "You don't know how much that means to me," she said, removing her SIM card from her phone.

I realized what she was doing and followed her lead. I took my cell phone out of my purse and removed my SIM card as well. "I say we start over out here as new people with new lives. Hell, if we go back to the States, we got everything to lose. Out here, we got everything to gain."

At that, Si-Si wiped the tears that seemed determined to break free from her eyes. She raised her arm and threw her phone and SIM card out into the sea, as if she were pitching for the major leagues. I followed suit. Then we both turned to walk into Andrew's private suite inside the Fiera di Genova. Italy had no idea what Si-Si and I were about to do to it. The takeover had officially begun.

November 2007

"Uh, uh, ah, uh. Oh, my God, Andrew, Andrew! Oh, please, please! Yes, Andrew, yes, yes, baby! Please!" I woke up to the sound of some chick stroking Andrew's ego while he was apparently stroking her. I thought the sounds were just in my dreams at first, which was why I didn't get up right away. But when I realized I hadn't been dreaming, I got right out of bed and walked over to the door of my bedroom. It was dark, so I walked extra slow and careful, with my hands out in front to help guide me. It was only my second night at Andrew's three-bedroom town home in an area called Monteverde Vecchio. For the two weeks following the boat show up until the other night, Si-Si and I stayed with Andrew at his nine-bedroom villa on Lake Bracciano outside of Rome. Once we had a sit-down with him and told him we wanted to see what it was like living out here, he brought us to his town home closer to the city to see if we wanted to live in it until we found something of our own. He even promised he would stay here with us until we felt secure and comfortable staying alone. He didn't say anything about bringing company, though. But it was his name on all the bills so I guessed he didn't have to.

I crept down the hall to the master suite. I pressed my ear up to the crack in the French doors. The moans and groans I heard in my sleep were louder and sounded crisper. I guessed it was Si-Si, but I couldn't really tell. And the longer I stood there listening to the lovemaking, the more turned on I got. After a while I wanted to go in and join them so bad. Instead, I tiptoed down the hall in the opposite direction toward Si-Si's room. I turned the knob. The door was locked. I tapped on it lightly a few times. A half-asleep Si-Si opened it with aggravation and concern written all over her face.

"Oh, I'm sorry to wake you, Si-Si," I whispered. "Never mind. Go 'head back to sleep."

"What's wrong?" Si-Si asked in a regular tone.

"Shhh," I put my index finger up to my mouth. I didn't want Andrew and his date to hear us and stop doing what they were doing. It was entertaining. Plus, I was so turned on by them, it was as if I was getting some too. It had been a while—a long while—since I had had sex, and I was beginning to remember just how much I missed it.

"Why?" Si-Si asked in a lower tone.

"Andrew is in there gettin' it on with some chick."

"For real?" Si-Si asked, confused and doubtful.

"Yeah. Her screaming is what woke me up. I thought it was you in there gettin' the business."

"You lyin'."

"Come hear for yourself," I said.

Si-Si followed me to Andrew's room. As we got down the hall, the sounds of the woman expressing her pleasure grew louder. Si-Si stopped short of the door.

"I feel disrespected," she said.

I turned to look at her. I was about to respond to her comment, but before any words could slip from my tongue, Si-Si barged into Andrew's room and flipped the light switch on his crystal chandelier.

"*Andrew!*" Si-Si shouted. "*What the hell are you doing?*"

"Sienna?" Andrew questioned, panting as he picked the blond-haired, big-boobed, thin-waisted girl up off his lap and placed her down on the mattress beside him. I smirked at the fact that she looked like the white version of Si-Si.

Andrew and the girl had a quick and intense game of tug-of-war for the sheets, trying hurriedly to cover their naked bodies.

"Is this your wife?" the girl asked Andrew, speaking with an American accent.

"No," he answered.

"*Is this your girlfriend?*" Si-Si asked.

"No," he answered again.

Meanwhile, I just watched, half shocked and half amused. I never expected Si-Si to react in that way. I mean, since we had gotten to Italy, she and Andrew never expressed any commitments to each other. They didn't have sex. They didn't even kiss. So how could she feel disrespected? From what she told me, Andrew had been a client of hers when she used to work as an escort. A relationship like that meant no strings attached. What had changed, I didn't know.

"*Then what is she doing here? In your bed? With your dick in her ass?*"

Yes, the girl was giving it to Andrew from the back, but there was no way for us to know if he was sticking her in the butt. Si-Si was just exaggerating at that point.

"Sienna, what is your problem? I can have someone over if I want. This is my house." Andrew explained himself, even though simultaneously stating that he didn't have to.

"Yes, it's your house! But I'm in it! Couldn't you have chosen a time and day when I was nowhere around?"

"For what?" Andrew asked.

"Out of respect for me!"

"Sienna, we don't have a relationship. And what we did have disappeared after you told me how old you really were and how you were forced into the business and everything! I felt bad for you. I felt like I was participating in something cruel, something wrong. I couldn't look at you the same after that! I mean, we're friends, and we'll always be, but . . ."

Si-Si was silent.

"Should I go?" The girl took that opportunity to try to make her escape.

Andrew, clearly frustrated, huffed and said, "Yes, maybe you should."

He fumbled around under the covers for a bit, then emerged from the bed with a pair of boxers on. He leaned over and picked up a pair of jeans that had been tossed on the floor. He dug into the pockets and pulled out a wad of euros. I counted as he peeled off six banknotes, each one a 500-euro bill.

"Here's your tip," he said, handing the girl the currency.

Tip, I thought to myself. Three thousand euro, and that's just the tip? What the hell? I woulda fucked Andrew for that kind of money.

Andrew left the girl to get dressed and walked toward us. On his way by he grabbed Si-Si's arm and pulled her out the room with him. Si-Si didn't resist. She walked with Andrew downstairs to the kitchen. I followed them. I was nosy.

They sat at the table, and I sat at the counter. No one said anything at first. Andrew just rubbed his hand over his head full of curls and looked up at Si-Si with forgiving but disturbed eyes.

Si-Si finally broke her silence. "What agency?" she asked, attitude still lingering.

Andrew hesitated and gave her a what-does-it-matter look. Si-Si shot him a nigga-answer-the-question look, and he said, "Emperor's VIP Club. Why?" He shrugged his shoulders.

Si-Si was silent again. She rolled her eyes and started shaking her leg. Her arms were folded across her chest.

Andrew reached out and placed his hand on her leg, trying to stop it from shaking.

"Sienna, what's the matter?" he nearly whined. It was evident he had a soft spot for Si-Si.

She looked at him and took a deep breath. "I won't be mad," she said with a sigh.

Andrew's body language spoke relief.

"But," Si-Si said, causing him to tense up again, "I want in."

Andrew turned his palms up and raised his shoulders. "What do you mean?"

"I want to know who owns the club, where it's run out of, and all the money details."

"And how do you expect me to get you that information?" he asked, as if doing so was impossible.

"Go upstairs to the source," Si-Si said matter-of-factly. "Bring her down to me. I'll get it."

Andrew shook his head and reluctantly got up from the table. He walked past me and headed upstairs.

As soon as he left, Si-Si turned to me. She started laughing.

"What the hell is so funny? What are you about to do to that poor man?"

"The other day we were asking ourselves how we were

going to make our own money out here, right?" Si-Si recollected.

"Yeah," I confirmed.

"Well, I'm about to put you on some real money," she said, her eyes gleaming. "We goin' open our own version of the Emperor's VIP Club, or whatever it's called, right down here."

"So that's what that whole scene was about?"

"You didn't think I was jealous, did you?" Si-Si smirked. "Andrew can bring an escort in here all he wants. But best believe I'm goin' network with the bitch."

"Well, damn, Si-Si, how did you know the girl was an escort? What if she was his girlfriend, or what if she was a chick he had bagged at a club?"

"If she was his girl, we would've been introduced to her a long time ago, or at least known of her," Si-Si responded. "Plus, escorts are Andrew's twist. He once told me that of all things in the world, sex was the best thing his money could buy." Then she added with confidence, "I knew what I was doin'."

I laughed. "You are crazy! But smart." I gave Si-Si her credit.

That night Si-Si drilled the girl, who happened to be a top girl in the very business Si-Si was in when she'd first met Andrew. She found out that the escort service the girl worked for was New York–based and had quite the clientele list, from über-rich businessmen to well-known politicians. Si-Si knew all the right questions to ask, and from the girl's responses, she was able to put together a business plan in her head. She was bad. Andrew and I both were impressed.

After the Q&A, Si-Si demanded the girl get the owner of

the club on the phone. She knew the girl had direct access to the owner because she'd said there was no way he would let one of his top girls go on a date out of the country without their being able to get in touch at the drop of a hat. And when the nervous girl said she didn't want to call the boss at one A.M., Si-Si was quick to point out that it was only seven P.M. in New York. The girl gave in and punched in a number on her cell phone.

Andrew sat with his hands folded under his chin and his elbows resting on his knees. He was still in his underwear but by then had added a white robe as well.

I was next to him, facing Si-Si, who was beside the girl on the couch across from us.

We all waited while the phone rang.

"Put it on speaker," Si-Si said.

The girl did.

"Hello," a male's voice answered.

"Ry, it's me, Dana," the girl spoke into the phone.

"What's up? Everything all right?"

Si-Si's face wrinkled as she seemed to be straining to hear.

"Give me the phone," she said, her hand out.

Dana, with the same exact worried look on her face that she had when Si-Si caught Andrew and her fucking, passed Si-Si the phone.

"Hello," Si-Si said, talking directly into the phone's built-in mic.

"Who's this?" the voice quizzed.

I know this voice, she mouthed to us, then she spoke into the phone once more. "It's Sienna." Nothing was heard from the other guy. In that moment of silence, Si-Si stood up from the couch. Her facial expression went from one of confusion to one of anticipation, and she asked, "Is this who I think it is?"

Still nothing from the other end.

"Ryan?" Si-Si asked, cracking a smile. "Ryan, if it's you, just say so!" she said excitedly.

"Sienna?" the voice returned.

Si-Si screamed, "Oh, my God!"

Andrew, Dana, and I were watching Si-Si as if we were watching a movie, waiting almost impatiently for what would happen next.

"Who is that, Si-Si?" I asked.

With a huge smile on her face she exclaimed, "This is my got damn brother!"

All of us, especially Dana, were shocked to learn that the owner of this escort service was Si-Si's brother. The world couldn't get no smaller.

She got back on the phone and giddily started asking him basic questions. "How have you been?"

"Maintaining," he responded.

"In a big way, I see," she said, still smiling. "You finally pinned down your dream."

"I see I'm not the only one. Miss Superstar, Si-Si Alvarez."

"I take it you watch TV."

"Enough to know what's going on around me."

"So you heard?" Si-Si asked, then she took the phone off speaker and headed upstairs to continue her conversation. I followed her. She took the girl's cell phone and all.

"I did what I had to, and I'll explain when I see you," Si-Si said into the phone as she climbed the stairs and walked down the hall toward her room.

I nudged her and mouthed, *What are you telling him?*

She mouthed back, *He's cool. Trust me.* Then she returned to her conversation.

"Yes, I'm gonna see you. Matter fact, I'm gonna check on a flight out here right now. We have a lot to talk about. And I wanna see you!" She bounced around her room like a teenage girl gossiping on the phone with her best friend.

Her comfort level with her brother was satisfying. If she trusted him, so did I. I let her continue talking to him without further interruption. They went on for hours. At one point Si-Si even came downstairs to ask Dana for her phone charger.

Meanwhile, Andrew wound up making us all the quintessential Italian breakfast—frittatas, which are like unfolded omelets, crusty bread with a chocolaty hazelnut spread called Nutella, and cappuccinos. The four of us ate and drank and talked about the possibilities of starting our own escort service until five o'clock the next morning. Then we managed to sleep our recommended eight hours and get up in time to dress and be at the airport by three p.m. Not only did we have to drop Dana off for her five p.m. flight back to New York, but Andrew, Si-Si, and I had to pick up Ryan.

After talking to each other on the phone, Si-Si and Ryan were both excited about his coming to see her right away. He'd booked a flight immediately.

Si-Si couldn't stand still as we waited at baggage claim for Ryan to show up. She was filled with excitement. I was eager to meet him just off her enthusiasm. A crowd of people came toward the carousel, and Si-Si eyed each person. She let out a scream and burst into tears when a tall, muscular, Tiger Woods look-alike appeared in the crowd. She jumped into his arms. Even he grew teary-eyed. Apparently, the two of them had a strong bond. Again I stood on the sidelines and watched with admiration as Si-Si reunited with another handsome man for whom she had a lot of love. I longed for my turn to come when I could be reconnected with the passion and security I could get only from a man. And as I felt myself grow a tiny bit jealous, I shook the feeling. My time will come, I thought.

Ryan exchanged brief words with Dana before she had to go on to her gate.

"I'll see you when I get back, which will probably be in a couple months. Everything is still going to run the same though—"

"Oh wow, we have you for that long?" Si-Si butted in.

Ryan focused his attention on Si-Si for a second. "It's goin' to take at least that long to set things up out here. I mean, unless that's a problem."

"Of course not," she said. "I'm thrilled!"

Ryan smirked, and it was something in that brief interaction between Si-Si and him that struck me as odd. I understood that they hadn't seen each other in a long time and were happy to reunite, but their chemistry was a little too strong for them to be brother and sister, if you ask me.

Ryan caught himself and stopped staring at Si-Si, then turned his attention back to Dana. "M.B. has your money. Get home safe."

The girl nodded and went on her way. Then Ryan's attention shifted to us. First he and Andrew shook hands.

"Nice to finally meet you." Ryan sized Andrew up.

"The pleasure is mine, buddy," Andrew said, returning the size-up.

Ryan then turned to me with his hand out.

"Celess," I said, placing my hand in his.

"Nice to meet you as well," he said with a smile that revealed dents in his cheeks that were too sexy to be called dimples.

His soft but firm handshake sent shock waves through me, and I swore his eyes were on my cleavage a little longer than they should have been. Maybe my time was going to come sooner than I thought. Suddenly, I shared Si-Si's joy. Brother or not, this nigga was so sexy and mesmerizing, I would be overexcited about seeing him too.

We all left the airport and got into Andrew's Rolls-Royce Phantom stretch limousine. The driver pulled away from the curb, and we were off to Andrew's town home to map out the plans we'd been discussing since late the previous day. I was supposed to be focused on business, but the whole ride all I could think about was how I was going to use Ryan to relieve my sexual tension. I knew mixing business with pleasure could lead to disaster. But it's been said that only after disaster can we be resurrected. And my sex life damn sure needed to be risen from the dead.

December 2007

I was in Andrew's home office browsing the Internet to see what the headlines were back home. Si-Si and I had done that quite frequently to make sure we were staying off the radar. I checked all the national news sites as well as the international ones. I even checked the popular blog sites. Only one thing stood out in my search and it was from a blog called panachereport.com. I swear the chick who does that blog was talkin' about Si-Si and me in one of her blind items. It said, "Two Hollywood vixens ditched their rising film careers to start an exclusive escort business overseas." I don't know how the hell she got her information, but her sources are a muthafucka, I thought. I was just glad she hadn't exposed us entirely and named names, like most bloggers would have. Then it would have been a problem.

But other than that we were in the clear. Most of the news stories surrounded the war in Iraq, the upcoming presidential campaign, and the writer's strike. It seemed Si-Si and I had left California at just the right time. Had we stayed there, we would have been broke. It was hard enough getting film and TV work when writers *weren't* on strike.

Anyway, I was just about to shut down the computer when Si-Si walked in.

"Whatchu doin'?" she asked as she walked around the desk and stood behind me.

"Checking the news," I said, closing the laptop.

"Anything I should know?"

"One blog mentions us," I said.

"WHAT?" Si-Si asked, alarmed.

"Not like that," I said.

"Then like what?" Si-Si's concern level remained high.

"I think we were one of her blind items."

"Who, panache report?" Si-Si hit it.

"Yeah. How you know?"

"She famous for her blind items," Si-Si said. "What did she say?"

I recited to Si-Si what the blog had. And her reaction was the same as mine.

"Well at least she didn't say too much. She could've dove a lot deeper."

"Exactly," I said. "So we should be good."

"Anything else?" Si-Si asked.

"No, thank God. Just that the writers are still on strike, so don't be expectin' no gigs to come through," I joked.

Si-Si smirked and said, "The gig we are about to get knocks all of them down tenfold. My brother's booker made a milli last year."

"Wow, so imagine what your brother made as the owner. What's a booker?"

"That's the person who connects the clients with the girls and books all the dates. It's the position Ryan was working his way up to when we were in the same house. And now he's the boss. I'm proud of him. I always knew he had it in 'im," Si-Si explained as she reminisced.

"Quick question," I said, figuring it was the right time to bring up my concern. "Wasn't your disgust for the whole escort business the reason you ratted your boss out and had his whole shit shut down? And if so, with that being the case, why would you wanna get into that same line of work?"

"It wasn't the business that bothered me. It was the business practices. Chatman used to force girls into the trade. I would never do that. There's plenty who will willingly and gladly come on board."

"Ohhhh." I understood.

"Plus, that bastard had my father killed, and he lied to me about my mom. What I did to him was light compared to what he did to me."

"Right. So you're saying that, without forcing anybody into the business, and of course without any shady shit, this is the best bet for us? You feel like this is the venture we should put our all into?"

"Absolutely," Si-Si said with a high degree of confidence. "It's so lucrative. I mean, anytime Andrew puts his money behind something . . . He's a moneyman—all business. Anything and everything he does revolves around how much it will make him."

"Well, you know what you're doing, so I'm goin' follow your lead. And I haven't seen you this motivated to do something since I met you and you quit your job on the spot. So that tells me you feel strongly about this."

"It's what I know. I was raised in this business. Ryan and me both. And to have him involved makes it all the better.

Like, I couldn't ask for a better partner. We used to dream about owning a business like this together, and here we are after all those years of being apart about to do it. I feel like it's meant. The timing is so right. Down to the fact that the economy in the States got Andrew needing to move his money into other businesses. His being willing to back us financially is the icing on the cake. And he not only has enough liquid assets to fund the entire venture, but he's connected to some of the richest people in the world. So we got a database of potential clientele at our fingertips. There's no way we can fail."

"Well, look, I'm with it. Shit, we gotta start making our own money somehow. And everything about this idea is falling into place perfectly, so why go against the grain?"

"Exactly. Why complain on easy street?"

At that, I put my hand up for Si-Si to slap it. She did. Then she instructed me to get dressed.

"For what?" I asked. "I was about to go to bed."

"Ryan, Andrew, and I are taking you out for your birthday," she sprang on me.

"My birthday isn't for another five days."

"We know, but Andrew will be away then. Besides, tonight is not just about celebrating, it's about business. Andrew got invited to this guy's club who's knee-deep in the business. He said we could scout new clients. He invited the cream of the crop. A shark pool. We gotta work the room. Give them a taste of what they'll get if they join our club."

"So you sayin' I can finally get me some tonight?" I was hopeful.

Si-Si shot me a malicious grin and said, "Put ya freak-'em dress on!"

Andrew had given his driver the night off because it was his anniversary, and rather than call another one at short notice, he decided we would take two cars out. The guys would take the Bugatti, and Si-Si and I would take the Ferarri.

It was a quarter after midnight when Andrew, Ryan, Si-Si, and I pulled up to a club called Diva Futura Channel Club. The minute we stepped out of our cars, all heads turned one way. You would've thought it was the pair of exotic cars that brought on the sea of eyeballs, but after the valet had parked the vehicles, men and women were still staring at Si-Si and me, some of them couldn't even close their mouths. It was to be expected, though. I was sure we were the only girls going in the basement-type strip club wearing shit straight off the runway. Si-Si had on a teal metallic Valentino spaghetti-strapped minidress—one from his last ready-to-wear collection. It was ruched at the bustline, allowing her boobs to scream for attention. It draped just a little from the hip to the middle of her thigh, where it stopped. The hemline looked like the top of an upside-down tulip. She wore matching teal and fuschia–striped open-toe heels and a big fuschia Valentino purse.

I wore a sequined Emilio Pucci shift dress in black and various shades of gold. It came to the middle of my thigh. It had long sleeves that were open and dangled loosely like flags from a flagpole. I paired it with some simple peep-toe black patent-leather Louboutins. I carried a black leather clutch, also Louboutin.

We got to the door, and one of the bouncers noticed Andrew right away.

"Andrew, *amico mio, come butta,*" the stocky dark-skinned Italian guy said as he motioned for Andrew to walk up to the front of the line.

Andrew grabbed hold of Si-Si's hand and led her to the front. I was right behind her, and Ryan was behind me.

"*Come sei*, Dominic," Andrew said, shaking the guy's hand. "We're here to see Marco."

"Yeah, I know. He's waiting on you," the guy said as he stepped to the side to let us in.

We didn't pay or get searched like the other patrons, and I guessed it was because either Andrew's money gave him power or he was a regular at the club. It was probably both, and maybe more of the latter. Hell with making it rain, Andrew was probably known for bringing hurricanes through that muthafucka. He was single, superrich, and he loved a woman he could pay for.

As we walked through the club over to a roped-off section in the corner, all our eyes, including Si-Si's and mine, were on the various naked foreign girls who decorated the club. I didn't know about anyone else, but I felt myself getting turned on almost instantly. There is something about a woman's naked body that makes me want to have sex. And it isn't that I'm sexually attracted to women because, if that were the case, I would not have changed my sex to become one. But there was something there. I just didn't quite understand what it was.

"Marco," Andrew greeted a tall, slim, but nicely built guy, with a well-groomed goatee and smooth skin that glowed.

The guy stood up from the cozy bench, and he and Andrew exchanged pecks on each cheek.

"*Ciao*." The guy acknowledged the rest of us.

"Marco, Sienna. Sienna, Marco," Andrew said, beginning the introductions with Si-Si.

"*È un piacere incontrario*," Si-Si said, her hand inside his.

"*Parlate Italiano?*" Marco asked, a surprised look on his face.

Andrew cut in and said, "She's pretty well versed. But her friends speak English."

I guessed Andrew didn't want any long-drawn-out conversations to take place in Italian and make Ryan and me uncomfortable.

"Oh, okay. And who are your friends, by the way?"

"Celess," I spoke up, giving Marco my hand.

"Beautiful name, Celess," he said.

"Thank you."

"And you?" He looked at Ryan.

"I'm Ryan. Nice to meet you." They shook hands.

After the introductions we all sat down, and immediately a topless cocktail waitress brought us a couple bottles of champagne and glasses.

"So, Andrew, *che cosa è nuovo?* I hear you're crossing over to the wild side, my friend."

I whispered to Si-Si, whom I ended up sitting next to, "What did he say?"

"What's new," she whispered back, her eyes staying on Andrew and Marco.

"Well, I don't know about that. I'm just trying to move some money around. You know, with the way things are going in America—"

"Headed for financial crisis, right?"

"There's a whole lot going on over there. I just want to move some money before it takes effect, you know."

"Of course you do. So you're looking to start a service agency? What made you want to get into this industry," he asked, his palms facing up as if he's showing off the place. "You seem so square. Please tell me. I'm all ears."

Andrew chuckled and said, "Well, we all know the definition of *seem*."

We all chuckled briefly. Then Andrew continued, "No, really, though. I've always been interested in the business. You see, Sienna here, I've known her for a long time. I actually met her in the business. We used to do our thing, you know, and then for some years we been apart. Just recently she came out here from the States just to visit, and, uh, a funny story, that I won't get into right here, right now—"

"Why not?" Marco cut Andrew off. "Funny stories usually turn into success stories. Do tell."

Andrew glanced at Si-Si. She motioned for him to go ahead and tell the story.

"Okay, then," Andrew started. "I had a vice girl over from America, and, well, we were, you know—"

"Fucking." Marco aided Andrew. "You were fucking."

We all chuckled at Marco's candor, as it was more entertaining than Andrew's elusiveness. Maybe he needed to loosen up, I thought. And feeling the need to loosen up myself, I took a sip of champagne.

"Yeah, basically." Andrew was still vague, "Anyway, the girls heard me, and Sienna, here, barged in. Right away she demanded to know everything—where the girl was from, who owned the agency she worked for, so forth and so on, and getting all that information led us to the idea of starting a service of our own."

"I'm sure there's more to be told, but funny nonetheless," Marco said, then chuckled briefly. "So what's the story with you all? Are you all fucking or something? Couples? What is this?" Marco sipped his champagne.

Everybody chuckled except me. I started to fantasize about Ryan.

Then, interrupting my thoughts, Marco added, "Are you guys gay or something? Why aren't you banging these two? They're drop-dead gorgeous."

Andrew defended his manhood and replied, "Sienna used to service me." He was inching toward being blunt.

"Past tense?" Marco inquired.

"We do better as business partners," Andrew came back.

"Oh, well what about her?" he looked at me. "She looks like a supermodel from one of the Paris shows."

I smiled at Marco with both my mouth and my eyes. I had a weakness for men who paid me high compliments.

"Celess, here, is Sienna's friend from the States. They met in California, in the movie business—"

"Adult-movie business?" Marco wanted details.

Si-Si cut in, "Something like that."

"Okay." He nodded, looking at us both, seemingly imagining us in an adult movie. "And you, my man." He extended his hand out toward Ryan. "Where do you fit into the picture? Or are you first in line to pay for one of these American beauties?"

There was another chuckle across the board. Then Ryan cleared his throat and sat up. "I'm one of the owners of a prominent club based in New York City," Ryan said proudly, with a bit of arrogance even. He made my nipples perk up. "I'm also Sienna's brother," he added.

"Oh, I see." He looked Ryan in the eyes for some seconds longer than normal. Then he commented, "You're keeping it in the family? The way I like it."

"And, Andrew, I take it you're just funding this thing, *giusto*?"

"Yes, that's correct. But also I'll be active in a lot of the dealings. I mean, clearly I'm no stranger to the business—I've been on both sides. From patronizing to—"

"Pimping." Marco grinned.

We all shared another laugh. It was as if we were at a comedy club.

"In so many words." Andrew was determined to hold on to his modesty.

"Well, I guess you're wondering why I asked to meet with you . . ." He sipped his champagne.

Andrew nodded.

"I hear you're looking for a venue for your agency. And, well, let's be real, you wouldn't be looking to house these girls if you know like I know, so that leaves one other option—a club. And if you open a club, then . . . Let's just say, I don't want to compete against you, and I'm sure you wouldn't want to compete against me. I mean, we can both have successful businesses, but one of us is gonna come in second place no matter what. Why not just partner?"

Andrew expressed his comprehension with a head nod, but he didn't say anything. He sat up and looked around the club some. He nodded again but was still quiet.

Meanwhile, Marco's brown deep-set eyes looked through Ryan, Si-Si, and me, as if he had X-ray vision. He rubbed his goatee a couple times. He even did a neck roll. Then he added, "You'll save so much time and money—the two most important things to men like you and me. You go spend, what, sixty days searching for a venue, then another thirty closing on it. Or even if you buy it outright, you spend a few million out of pocket before you make a single dime. Then there's another thirty to sixty days to get licenses, and then you still need time to fix it up to your liking. But here, you have an establishment that will cost you nothing up front. I only get paid when you do. And I'll only charge you fifteen percent, five less than the going rate. You could launch your agency today and start making money tomorrow. It's already up and running." Then, after a brief pause, he said, "I don't know why you didn't come to me first anyway—"

"I actually thought about you," Andrew said. "I did. I was hesitant, though, about bringing something like this to you after Riccardo and Eva being sentenced for the whole prostitution-ring thing—"

Marco butted in. "That happening makes this situation all the better . . ."

Andrew's face wrinkled with curiosity.

"Who're Riccardo and Eva?" I whispered to Si-Si.

"I don't know, but we gotta google them first thing," Si-Si whispered back, rushing the last couple words so that she could continue to pay attention to Marco's proposal.

Marco continued, "You see, with them being away, I could use an extra stream of income. Plus, seeing as though I was around to witness the mistakes they made, I'll be able to steer you all away from making those same mistakes and following down that same road," Marco sensibly explained, raising his glass of champagne to his thin lips and taking another swig.

That triggered Ryan to sip his, then Si-Si, then me. Andrew sat still, listening intently to Marco's proposal.

Marco took advantage of Andrew's listening, and he kept right on talking. "Here's what I will tell you," he said. "There is so much money to be made in what you want to do. But if not done right, there is so much more heartache to be stood. And I know the right and wrong way. You can't have illegal immigration, no abuse, and no drugs. If you're in it, be in it to sell pussy, not slaves. *Capisce?*"

"*Capisco,*" Andrew agreed. "You do have experience in

this business. And a reputable venue already. And that's all we need." He rubbed his hands together and concluded, "Let me sleep on it. Let's party. Celebrate Celess's birthday. And then come back to this in a few days or so." Andrew wrapped the meeting up in a nice bow.

Marco uncrossed his legs and sat up.

"I like that you suggest that, Andrew, but I should tell you, as a businessman and an investor, you shouldn't sleep on anything. You can miss an opportunity in a blink of an eye. So imagine how many opportunities you would lose with your eyes closed for eight hours?"

"You got a point," Andrew said.

Marco proceeded. "What do you need from me to be able to give me an answer right now?"

Andrew looked to us. Si-Si nodded. Ryan followed. I just smiled. I didn't know or care either way. I trusted they did, though. This was their thing. I was just along for the ride and would play my part when needed.

"I can say yes to joining you and using your venue and, of course, hearing some guidance. And I'm prepared to say yes. I just need to know that I can trust you, Marco."

"Trust me? With what? Your money? I have enough of my own right now. Your livelihood? The livelihood of a partner of mine is like my own livelihood. I jeopardize yours, I jeopardize mine. Your freedom? Well, that's the one thing you can't put in my hands. I'm not God. But I will say this, I am a man of my word, and never has my word gotten anybody into trouble with the law or otherwise. I am no rat. Andrew, you know this, when Italians do business with people, we expect certain things from those people. We expect loyalty. We expect integrity. And we expect commitment. You see, we don't just do business with people. We get into bed with them. It becomes a marriage. 'Til death do us part. And when our names are on the line and our reputations and our freedoms, we take that very, very seriously. So as long as you and your partners here apply those principles to this, then you have absolutely nothing to worry about."

"*Capisco*, one hundred percent. In that case, it's a yes," Andrew said. "And just so you know, Marco, this isn't something I just thought to do overnight. I've wanted to do it many years ago. And I even dibbled in it a little when I used to set things up with Sienna on the side. I just never had the right people around me to pursue it. But now, with the way Sienna and her brother came full circle like this, and with you approaching me to provide a venue, I feel like it's time."

"And timing is everything," Marco said, grabbing the champagne flute that sat on the table in front of him and lifting it in the air. "*Cin cin*," he said.

After the waitress refilled the empty glasses, we picked them up, leaned in, and toasted.

Marco lowered his glass from his mouth and turned to Andrew. "First thing in the morning, let's draw up a contract."

Andrew nodded in agreement.

Then Marco turned to Si-Si and me and said, "In the meantime, there are some people you girls need to make friends with."

At that, Marco stood up and pointed out a few potential clients for Si-Si and me to get to know.

As we headed over to them, he stopped us in our tracks.

"That one," he pointed to a white-haired, fragile old white guy. "*Ricco sfondato*."

"Ricco who?" I asked Si-Si.

"*Ricco sfondato*," she repeated. Then, her eyes on the prize, she translated, "Rolling in money, endlessly rich."

She sasshayed over to the old guy ready to work. It reminded me of how she was when I sent her in the gym for the first time to snag Corey, our personal trainer back in L.A. who accepted sex as payment. And the same feeling I had back then returned. I felt like a proud mom watching her offspring take on an amazing challenge. I let the feeling resonate for a short while, then I got focused. Momma had some business to take care of of her own. I touched up my lipstick and gloss, adjusted my cleavage, and headed over to a middle-aged darker-skinned white guy. Let the good times roll, I said to myself.

Si-Si and I paraded around the club like we owned it, conversing with and wooing our prospects. We flirted a lot, got drunk as hell on the house, and gave out countless lap dances. By the time the club closed, we had a whole Rolodex of clientele, and I was so drunk and horny I woulda fucked any one of them on the spot—free of charge. But I didn't want to compromise our newly formed business relationship with Marco. I wasn't *that* drunk.

"All right, there's no way you two can ride home together. Neither of you is in any condition to drive," Andrew said, holding Si-Si up by her upper arm. "So who's riding with who?"

Si-Si was getting ready to say something, but before the words could slide off her drunken tongue, Ryan suggested, "Why don't you two go ahead and ride together. I'll drive Celess."

I was not at all surprised at Ryan's offering to ride with me. This would be his first opportunity to get me alone since he'd moved in with us three weeks ago. And I could tell he had been wanting to. He flirted with me every chance he got, but between him running his business, helping us start ours, and being surrounded by Si-Si's and Andrew's eyes and ears, there was no way he could sneak it in. But it was no secret he wanted me. And what was less of a secret was the fact that Si-Si didn't necessarily like it. A few days after Ryan had arrived, she'd vaguely told me that he was off limits to me. I asked her why, and she said she had her reasons. I laughed it off. But I noticed how she never left us alone and always emphasized his dealings with other chicks—whenever Andrew would bring one home for him. I planned to get to the bottom of her overbearing behaviors pertaining to Ryan. But in time. My first priority was fucking him—at least once.

Si-Si was about to object to the idea of Ryan's driving me, but before she got the chance, Andrew said, "Perfect. Let's go."

We went outside, and the valet already had Andrew's cars at the door. Andrew helped Si-Si as she sat down in the passenger's seat of the Bugatti. The valet moved to close her door, and she stopped him.

"Ryan!" she called out.

Ryan, who was already sitting in the driver's seat of the Ferrari, got out of the car and jogged the few feet up to Si-Si.

"What's up?" he asked, standing in front of her.

She bent her pointer finger up and down, motioning for Ryan to come closer to her. He bent over and she whispered something in his ear. What is she telling him? I wondered. I know it's nothing about me, and I know it's not my secret, I hoped Si-Si's alcohol level, mixed with her objection to Ryan and me getting together, wouldn't lead her to betray me.

Ryan chuckled at whatever Si-Si told him, and I let out a sigh of relief. Si-Si didn't rat me out. If she did, Ryan's response would not have been a chuckle, believe me.

I undressed Ryan with my eyes as he returned to the Ferrari and slid into the driver's seat.

The valet then closed Si-Si's door, and Andrew sped away from the club. Ryan followed him.

"What was that about?" I asked Ryan. I was laid back in my seat, eyes halfway closed, with a permanent smile on my face.

"Nothing," he chuckled.

"Yeah, right," I said. "What did she tell you that was so funny?"

"Nothing. Just Sienna being Sienna."

"What does that mean? I never knew her to be a comedian."

"No, not a comedian. Just overprotective, and it happens to be funny."

"Overprotective? You're her brother, not her man."

Ryan laughed and said, "Ironically."

"What do you mean, ironically? What am I missing?"

"I take it she didn't tell you," Ryan began to let me in on something Si-Si had obviously been keeping hidden.

"Tell me what?"

Ryan smirked and looked at me. His slanted eyes so turned me on.

"It's a long story, believe me," he said.

I brushed it off. "Si-Si seems to have plenty of those. I guess I'll hear it one day." I didn't care what it was between the two of them. My hormones were out of control, and if I didn't settle them that night, I was bound to explode.

"Yeah, I'm sure you will," Ryan said, taking the hint that

I didn't want to get into the long story he referred to. "How did you meet Sienna anyway? You two seem like one in the same. I would've never guessed she would run into someone so much like herself."

Oh, my God, I thought to myself. Did he offer to be my designated driver so he could play twenty questions, or was he trying to have me to himself? I was starting to get frustrated at his beating around the bush.

"We met at a lingerie boutique," I lied, figuring I would go ahead and initiate. "I was buying some panties." I smiled, biting my bottom lip. I decided to go in for the kill, and I didn't care if I was coming off too strong or not. I was desperate, shit, and I was not too proud to beg. Besides, we were getting closer to the house, and I was determined to get some before we got there and Si-Si could spoil it.

"Oh, yeah?" he asked. The look on his face told me that he entertained the thought of my buying panties. "What kind of panties? Were they anything like the ones you have on now? Let me see them. See if I like them or not."

"I would show you," I said, "if I were wearing any."

I grabbed Ryan's right hand from off the steering wheel and placed it on my inner thigh. I rubbed his fingers, imagining them entering me. I opened my legs for him to touch me higher, and he did. His fingers climbed my thigh like a spider and started stroking my clit. It still works, I thought of my fairly new vagina. Since my sex change a few years back, I had a fear that one day I was going to wake up and my pussy wasn't going to work. But it worked just fine that night, and I sat there in the passenger seat enjoying every moment of it.

I started rubbing my breasts and thinking about what it would be like if Ryan actually penetrated me. And between

the vivid thoughts and Ryan's touch, I found myself demanding he pull over.

"What we goin' tell Andrew and Sienna?" he asked, pulling the car into an empty parking lot.

"Tell 'em you stopped at a drugstore for some medicine for
me. We'll say I had a massive headache or some shit. Who
cares?"

Obviously, Ryan cared. He dialed Andrew's number from
my phone and repeated the script I gave him. I could tell
there was some hesitation from Andrew by Ryan's responses.
And when Andrew told Ryan he would pull over and wait for
us to catch up, Ryan acted like my phone had died and hung
up on him. He turned off both our phones and started un-
buckling his pants.

"Do you have a condom?" he asked.

I pulled one from my clutch and gave it to him. He rushed
it on, and then he pulled me on top of him.

"It's about damn time," I moaned as his meaty dick entered my craving pussy. "It's about damn time."

January 2008

I woke up in the Copacabana Palace Hotel on the beautiful beach of Copacabana in Rio de Janeiro. We had been working nonstop on our business: hiring girls, putting up the Web site, opening an offshore account. We hadn't had any playtime. So Andrew suggested we come here to take a break, and he said it was one of the best places in the world to celebrate New Year's.

Si-Si had wanted to bring the new year in in Sydney, Australia, just so that we could be the first mothafuckas to say Happy New Year, but she lost the coin toss. I'm so glad she did. Nothing could have beaten the spectacular fireworks shown on the beach and the positive energy given off by the Brazilians and tourists alike. I mean, amid all the champagne and millions of people from different walks of life, not one fight broke out last night. Plus, my participating in the Brazilian ritual of sending lilies out into the sea in honor of Yemanjá, the Goddess of the Sea, bought me some much-needed peacefulness. I sent an additional lily out for my best friend, Tina. Her memory visited me the most on New Year's Eve—the anniversary of her death. And this time I tried embracing it rather than letting it sadden me.

We'd checked into our hotel at about six in the evening on New Year's Eve. We had the suite on the top floor with our own private pool, which we hadn't ever gotten into, by the way. We slept for about four hours after checking in, then got dressed for the festivities. Most people, including Andrew, were dressed in all white for luck. Si-Si opted to wear blue for peace, and I wore green for money. Go figure. Ryan decided to wear all three colors.

People had started gathering in front of our hotel and everywhere else along the beach at about nine. As it grew closer to midnight, the crowd grew exponentially.

The fireworks were aboard boats out in the ocean, and exactly at midnight they lit up the dark sky. The weather was equally beautiful, warm and clear. I had never experienced such a New Year's celebration. We drank and partied, and when the shows were over on Copacabana, we went over to Ipanema Beach and drank and partied some more. We didn't get back in our hotel suite until seven in the morning on New Year's Day.

I was sitting in the Jacuzzi tub eating a Snickers from the minibar and sipping a glass of Pinot Grigio when Si-Si barged into the bathroom.

"Let's go to Cape Town," she said, excited.

"How far is that from here?" I asked.

Si-Si burst into laughter and replied, "A plane ride. It's in South Africa."

"Hell, no!" I said, after learning that the bitch was not talking about a town in Brazil but a whole other country.

"Why not?" she squealed.

"Why so?" I asked.

"To finish off our New Year's celebration. I heard they do

it big down there on January 2. If we leave later today, we can get there in time."

"You lost your damn mind. I'm spent," I said.

"Aww, booooo," Si-Si said, sounding like an unhappy Apollo Theater audience member.

"I'm still tryin' to fully wake up," I explained.

"It's two in the afternoon!"

"Yeah, but after being in the air for eleven hours, sleeping for only a few, then being up partying for another ten, it's a wonder I'm up now!" I thought about how much more tired she should have been, and it prompted me to ask, "And how the hell are you so energetic?"

Si-Si smiled and said, "These caffeine Jell-O shots Ryan made. These bitches got me on. I can't sit my ass still."

I knew it had to be something. Si-Si was way too quirky.

"Well, shit, give me some!"

"You goin' go to Cape Town?"

"Ryan goin'?"

"Yeah."

"What about Andrew? What did he say about all this?"

"He don't care. He can write all this shit off. Plus, long as it's some pussy in Cape Town, Andrew is there!"

"Did he get some last night?" I asked, grinning.

Si-Si nodded. "Of course!"

"What about you? Did you fuck that chocolate Brazilian who had your ass hostage on the dance floor?" I asked reflectively.

"Indeed!" she said, "And I think Ryan got some too." She was sure to point this out.

"So I'm the only one who missed out?" I let the shit about Ryan roll right off my shoulders. Maybe Si-Si didn't understand Ryan was just a fuck buddy as far as I was concerned. I couldn't care less about him otherwise.

"If memory serves me correctly, I never seen you sneak off to the bathroom with nobody."

"Y'all some hoes!" I teased.

"So is that a yes or a no, so I can tell Andrew to gas up the Cessna."

"Fuck it. Tell 'im to gas up!" I put my glass of wine down and ate the last of the Snickers. I got out of the tub, stepped into the shower, washed, and got out. When I did, there were three bright red Jell-O shots lined on the marble countertop waiting for me.

"How many milligrams are in these things? Y'all fuck around and have me overdose!" I yelled out to Si-Si and Ryan.

"Only a hundred," Ryan yelled back. "The same amount that's in a one-ounce espresso!"

I took the shots and got dressed. In no time, we were at the Galeão International Airport headed for Cape Town, South Africa. I wanted to sleep on the flight, but I couldn't. Those damn Jell-O shots had me wired—Si-Si and me both. So while Andrew and Ryan caught up on rest, we talked.

"What are you thinking about?" I asked Si-Si, who was staring out the window.

"What's going on in the world," she said nonchalantly.

"What you mean?"

"Well, our world," she said. "Our old world," she clarified.

"Oh, back in Cali?" I figured.

"Yeah. I wonder what everybody is doing. What they're talking about . . ." Then she chuckled, "I wonder if we ever got into *Playboy*."

I chuckled too, and said, "I be thinking about that stuff too. I wonder if my movie came out, and if it did, what it made. Somebody could owe me a check right now, and I wouldn't know."

"I think about David a lot too," Si-Si said. "Sometimes I get the urge to call him so bad."

"Yeah, I can imagine. Y'all were in love."

"I wish none of that bullshit ever happened. I wish my grandma never died and nobody came and shot up her burial. I wish I could erase everything from then on," Si-Si said, gazing out the window.

"Yeah, I know. Me too. But in life I've learned that it's not what happens to you that matters but how you deal with it. And we are dealing with all that shit pretty good, if you ask me. Of course, we're still going to think and wonder. But at the end of the day we have to keep it moving. We can't dwell. Dwelling will hurt you. That shit will have you pick up an addiction or have you ready to kill yourself. I know that firsthand."

"I guess so," Si-Si said, turning away from the window.

"And just think, had we still been in L.A., we would not be on a plane to South Africa right now. We probably would be in Vegas somewhere, doing the same shit, seeing the same people."

"There is a bright side, isn't there?"

"In every situation."

"Well, thanks for always pointing it out to me. I need that sometimes," Si-Si said, reaching out to hug me.

I hugged Si-Si back, and she wiped a tear from the corner of her eye.

"We should toast," she said, waving to get the attention of the flight attendant.

miasha

"Can I have two glasses of champagne, please?" Si-Si asked the pale-skinned, blond-haired, blue-eyed young attendant.

"Sure. Would you two like dinner now as well?"

"What's being served?" Si-Si asked.

"Herbed beef tenderloin, or cold shredded lobster with mixed greens and a champagne fusion oil dressing."

"Ummm," Si-Si and I both moaned.

"It sounds good, but we should wait for the guys to wake up and eat with them." Si-Si was being considerate.

"Okay. Well, may I bring you an appetizer while you wait? We have sushi."

"No, thank you. But you can bring me another lobster shot."

"Me as well," I said, already tasting the vodka and herb-drenched pieces of lobster, which we had been greeted with the minute we were airborne.

"Sure," the flight attendant said, leaving our side.

Moments later she returned with our glasses of champagne.

Si-Si held her glass up and said, "Here's to the bright side."

I clinked her glass with mine and added, "Of every situation."

Si-Si nodded, and we took our sips.

"Celess, real talk, I appreciate you going through all this with me," Si-Si said sentimentally.

"Ain't like you wouldn't have gone through it with me."

"We are so much like the Italians," she chuckled.

"What, how we show loyalty?"

"Yes."

"We riders," I summed up our characters.

60

"'Til death do us part," Si-Si said, holding her glass up for another toast.

"'Til death do us part," I agreed, clinking her glass for the second time.

We sipped again and just sat back in our seats. I thought about Tina and how much Si-Si reminded me of her. Tina was tough and acted like nothing bothered her, but on the inside she was so emotional. That was Si-Si, and every so often she needed to be able to let out the emotions she kept caged inside her. My job was to allow her to do that. And that's just what I did, the same way when Tina used to retell me stories from her past, stories she had told me a million times before. Each time, I would just listen in silence as if that were the first time she had told it to me. That's what friends are for, I thought, simply to be there when they're needed. And that was one thing I was good at—I was good at being a friend. And if I didn't like anything about myself at all, that was the one thing I did like. I valued friendship and my ability to give it genuinely.

We landed in Cape Town at close to six in the morning. It was only a seven-and-a-half-hour flight from Rio de Janeiro, but because of the time difference it seemed like we'd been traveling longer.

We went straight to our hotel, and on the way there I was in awe looking at the sleeping city. The scenery resembled any one of America's cities—tall buildings, retail stores, and restaurants galore, nothing like the poor underdeveloped wastelands they show you on TV. I was surprised and even more so when we arrived at our hotel. Andrew booked us five-star accommodations at the Table Bay Hotel, Victoria & Alfred Waterfront.

It was a pastel yellow Victorian-style structure with baby blue rooftops. Tall palm trees lined the entry. Surrounding it were other pastel-colored Victorian-style buildings, all positioned in a seemingly perfect location offering dazzling views of the sea and mountains in the distance. The area—packed with restaurants, shops and boutiques, and arts and crafts stores—gave off an old-world charm blended with modern elegance. I actually felt like I was in a different world. The air was fresh and crisp. And the light rays of sunshine that referenced dawn bounced off the calm ocean, making the scene look like a painted seascape.

A wall of windows at the front entrance of the hotel provided a sneak preview of the dramatic décor in the massive lobby. A big beautiful flower arrangement sitting atop a round wooden glass-top table greeted us as we entered. Traditional furniture made the lobby feel like home. The parquet and marble floors were polished to a shine. I couldn't wait to see what our suite looked like.

The front desk clerk was very warm and welcoming as she checked us into our room. She gave us the keys and had a bellman take our luggage. The suite was everything I expected it to be, plus—spacious, striking, with glorious views. It looked like if we opened our window, we could reach our hands out to touch the ocean. Ships and yachts were as much a part of the room's background as the paint on the walls. It was surreal. The bathrooms were marble with separate showers. The turndown service was every bit the five stars the hotel boasted too. On the floor beside every bed was a pair of slippers surrounded by a few rose pedals.

It was by far one of the most luxurious hotels I'd ever stayed in. Who knew that Africa possessed such beauty and grandeur? I made a mental note to take plenty of pictures.

We didn't go right to bed like we had done when we first arrived in Rio de Janeiro. Instead, Andrew suggested we do breakfast at one of the hotel's restaurants. Neither Si-Si nor I were really hungry, but we were so excited to be in such a beautiful place that we couldn't sleep either, so we went with Andrew's suggestion.

"Hello," Andrew said into the room phone. "Everything is perfect, thank you. My party and I would like to have breakfast. Which restaurant is best? Okay, great. Thanks."

"Which one did they say?" Si-Si asked.

"The Atlantic Grill," Andrew said. "Supposedly they are known for having the best breakfast."

"Let's go then," Ryan said, rubbing his stomach, his shirt lifting a little in the process, revealing the bottom half of his sculpted abs.

We freshened up some and headed down to the Atlantic Grill. The buffet breakfast was extensive, including everything from homemade sausages to ostrich eggs. If Si-Si and I hadn't been hungry before, we were certainly hungry then.

We made our plates and sat at a table on the terrace. We ate our world-renowned breakfast as we watched the sun rise and claim the sky. The scenery took me back to a day several years ago when one of my exes, Tariq, had taken me out to the park. He was heavy into real estate, so he was reading one of those real estate books called *Rich Dad Poor Dad*. That day at the park he read me a quote about how the world is a playground for the rich. Sitting there in Cape Town after having been in Brazil just the day before made me realize how true that was. I wondered about Tariq and whether he was finally enjoying the world in such a way or had his world crumbled after he found out he was HIV positive. I said a quick prayer for him in my head. He was a good person. I hoped he was living his dreams, despite the unfortunate news he'd hit me with the last time we spoke.

After breakfast, we had dessert. Over our crème brûlée we played truth or dare just for laughs. Then, stuffed, we headed back to our suite. We rested up before it was time to get dressed and hit the streets.

Athlone Stadium was our first stop. It was where the Minstrel Carnival was held. Natives paraded in white-painted faces and larger-than-life costumes to the drumming of various marching bands. It reminded me of the Mummers Parade in Philly, only it symbolized the one and only day of freedom for slaves back in the nineteenth century.

The festivities continued throughout the day and into the night. Si-Si used the nonstop partying as an opportunity to get wasted. Ryan and Andrew scouted out a couple of African girls whom they could take back to the suite. And me, I soaked up the historical meaning behind the events. I told myself I would never let anyone or anything come between my freedom and me. No matter what. I realized then that that was the one thing more valuable than life itself. And I planned to treat it as such. I thanked God that I still had it, and seeing as though that fact was cause for celebration, I joined my friends and let loose. I helped myself to rounds of Bloody Mary shots until I couldn't stand up without help. By the end of the night we all were tore up.

Back at the hotel, I wound up passing out on the sofa. Si-Si somehow made it to her room with a gorgeous South African guy named Baruti. He told us his name meant educator, and he looked like he could teach me a thing or two. Si-Si was so lucky she got to his ass first.

Andrew had a girl in his room. And from what I remember, Ryan had one in his too. How Ryan and his girl ended up on the sofa with me is still a mystery. All I could recall was waking up to someone sucking my breasts so hard you would've thought milk was being produced for a starving newborn.

I forced open my eyes to find that the lips on my body belonged to Ryan. My initial thought was, What if Si-Si catches us? I tried to prop myself up on the arm of the sofa so that I could slip from beneath him, but my legs were pinned down. I looked past Ryan's head to get a glimpse of my lower body. That's when I realized the girl Ryan had brought to the hotel had her palms pressed firmly against my thighs, holding them open. And between them was her head. And when my brain had the chance to comprehend what was happening, it was like a chemical reaction had been set off. Out of nowhere I felt my clit receiving a kind of pleasure I had never experienced during sex before. I mean, I've heard that the tongue was the strongest muscle in the human body, but got damn. That girl's tongue was working overtime, giving me trembling spells and everything. It was like she was penetrating a nerve I never knew existed, and with the force of a cat licking her young clean.

Where a minute ago I had been ready to stop Ryan from proceeding to arouse me in my sleep, I was now begging him to keep going. And the fear of Si-Si or Andrew walking in on us deserted me. My mind had shifted gears. Instead of worrying about being caught, I found myself trying to figure out how I was going to get the girl to come back to Italy with me. I swear to God, I had to be sprung. Why the hell couldn't I have had an experience like that when I was still a boy, I thought. Because had a girl sucked me back in the day as good as that girl did, I was convinced I would not have been gay.

The day came for us to depart Cape Town, and although we all had had a blast, we were ready to return to Rome. Our business had officially launched, and we needed to be there to nurture it. Ryan explained that the first six months were crucial. They could either make you or break you. We needed to be booking girls as often as possible in that time period because that was when we would be baiting, hooking, and establishing a loyal clientele. If an agency was unable to obtain at least fifty loyal clients in its first six months of operation, then it was bound to fail.

We packed our belongings, which had nearly doubled after Si-Si and I went shopping at the V&A Waterfront. Andrew should have known better than to book us a hotel that was literally connected to a huge mall.

We got in the limousine that was waiting outside and we were off to the airport—Andrew, Ryan, Si-Si, myself—and Lisha, the girl with whom I had my first lesbian, or should I say straight, encounter. I managed to get my wish. I was bringing her ass back to Rome with us. Of course I didn't tell Andrew or Si-Si why. That was the secret Ryan, she, and I shared. What I did tell them was that she would be an asset to our agency. I wound up hiring her ass. And she didn't give a fuck either. Her words to me were, "Anything to get out of here."

We boarded the private plane, got comfortable in our seats, and took flight. No sooner did we land in Rome then Si-Si got a call from Diva Futura, home of our agency, Emperor's Club VIP: The Roman Empire, an addition we came up with that we felt was better than simply calling it Emperor's Club VIP II.

"*Ciao*," she answered the vibrating phone. After a momentary pause she exclaimed, "*Perfetto!*"

The look on Si-Si's face told me it was good news; besides, it didn't take a linguist to figure out that *perfetto* meant perfect.

"Who was that?" Ryan asked immediately after Si-Si hung up.

"It was Marco. We got our first request!"

"Already, huh?" Andrew asked, surprised.

"And guess what?" Si-Si grew more excited.

"What?" we asked in unison.

"It came from a famous soccer player . . . Ummm, Cris Ronaldo, or something like that."

"Cristiano? He's Manchester United's star player."

"Well, he just booked not one but two of our girls!" Si-Si said.

"Good stuff," Andrew said.

"Beginner's luck," Ryan followed up.

Si-Si and I screamed with excitement. It felt good to book our first date, and for it to have been with a fucking sports star was huge. That right there gave us so much confidence in our newfound business. Dollar signs were running a marathon through my head. We knew that drawing someone famous to our girls could give our agency just the attention it needed to make our quota. But none of us was prepared for the attention we were about to receive.

Somehow the tabloids got wind of Cristiano Ronaldo's rendezvous with our girls, and it was plastered all over the press that he had visited the Diva Futura Channel Club in

Rome and paid for two hookers to accompany him to his hotel. At first, we were devastated by the bad publicity, fearful that authorities would finish us before we even got started. But all it did was bring a slew of other customers our way, from the rich and famous to the average and nameless. By the end of January we had 170 customers, far exceeding our goal of fifty in six months. And just like that, our business took off, dragging our lifestyles, bank accounts, and what would turn out to be our problems right along with it.

February 2008

The sun lit up the sky and blanketed Rome with a warmth that isn't typical in February in many parts of the world. It was the first Thursday of the month. Si-Si and I had plans on starting the weekend already with a trip to Milan until Monday. We planned to drive up to do some shopping and just get away, but at the last minute we got a call from Marco. A customer wanted to book a date.

"Emperor's Club," Si-Si answered her cell. "We're actually all booked up, Marco," she informed him. "Oh, well, in that case, let me see what I can do."

Si-Si put her hand over the mouthpiece of the phone and repeated to me, "A guy wants just a day and will pay triple for the short notice."

"Well, go ahead then," I whispered to her.

"I was thinking you would go," she whispered. Then she got back on the phone. "Marco, either Celess or I will do it. Tell him he can check our pictures out on our site under the tab that says 'Wishful Thinking,'" Si-Si said. "He'll get one of the two girls there."

Si-Si told Marco she would call him back with details,

and she hung up. We had to decide which one of us would go on the date. I tried everything to get out of it and wished we hadn't booked all thirty-five of our girls. Even Lisha, our unofficial employee, was off on a date that day. I guessed a lot of our customers were trying to get their treats before they would be forced to spend Valentine's Day with their wives or girlfriends.

To decide who would take the date, we wound up doing what we always did to make this kind of decision: We flipped a coin. I chose heads, and three times out of five it landed on tails. I had to take the date. It was with a middle-age art collector who was in town from Florence for some art exhibition at the Palazzo Venezia. According to the copy of his driver's license that he faxed over, he wasn't bad looking. And much to my surprise, he was black. He actually resembled the actor Taye Diggs. Hmmm, tonight I might get my groove back.

I was in my room getting ready for the date. The house was silent and still. Ryan was out on a date—not like that. He stepped in as a driver for one of our girls who was booked for only two hours. I didn't know where Andrew was. Ever since he'd moved out of the town home and back into his villa, it had been hard for us to keep tabs on him. Si-Si was in her room. I believed she was calling around trying to get one of her male friends to take my train ticket and go to Milan with her. I was so jealous.

I traded my black Gucci leather military jacket, silver tights, and black Gucci booties for a yellow, black, and white knee-length Gucci skirt with oversize pleats. Up top I wore a black leather square-neck Gucci cardigan with hook-and-eye closures and a big black belt beneath my bustline.

I put on another pair of Gucci booties—black with yellow trimming—that tied and had a peep toe. I left my hair in a slicked-back ponytail, and I threw on a pair of black Gucci shades. Topping it off, I threw a black mink stole atop my shoulders. I went for the upscale, sophisticated look since I was going to an art exhibit.

"So," Si-Si's voice beat her to my room, "this'll be your first date. You nervous?"

"Nervous about what?" I asked. "If I know anything in this world, I know how to handle a man."

"Yeah, but this is different than what you're used to. These type men be wanting some weird shit sometimes. It's not like meeting a guy out somewhere, getting his number, then going to the hotel for a one-night stand. This is more like some man with a crazy fetish wants to pay me to do some kinky shit," Si-Si said.

"Key phrase is 'pay me,'" I said, unfazed by Si-Si's warning. "Long as he pay like he weigh, I'm good." I laughed.

Si-Si laughed a little too, but then she got serious. "No, but for real, though, you do need to know a few things," she began.

I remained silent.

"Don't go anywhere other than the place he said he was taking you to at the time of booking, which in this case is the Palazzo. If he decides to extend the date and wants to take you somewhere else, you have to let me know of the change—"

"What is the big deal? I mean, what if he wants to grab something to eat, or if I talk his ass into taking me shopping afterward?"

"It sounds like it's nothing to worry about, especially because you're grown, but this was the speech my boss gave me before my first date, and so I feel obligated to give it to you before yours. There are kidnappers in this business. And though they prey on minors mostly, you can't put it past them to take women too."

"What do you mean, take women? I'm not taken unless I wanna be. That's just that," I stated. Si-Si knew me better than that, and she knew that I held my own when it came to men. Why was she trying to scare me?

"I'm serious, Celess. I know you'll be all right. I mean, in the five years I worked in the business, from sixteen to twenty-one, I never experienced any problems like that. But it's better to be safe than sorry. The people who are pros in the sex trade know that there's a lot of money in selling girls. Just be aware of your surroundings and keep me posted of any change of events."

I nodded. "Okay, fine. It's just a few hours anyway."

I put on my YSL nude-colored lipstick and grabbed my gold Gucci pocketbook. I dumped everything from my silver Louis into it and headed for the door.

"What are you going to do while I'm gone?" I asked Si-Si as I was walking out the door.

She smiled and said, "Me and the guy Anthony and I met at the bank last month are going to Milan."

"I knew it," I said. "You ain't shit."

"I'm sorry," she whined. "I can't sit in here all day bored to death, and I don't want our tickets to go to waste."

"Just make sure you buy me as much shit as you buy yourself."

"No problem," she said. "And make sure you call me," she reiterated.

I got into the town car that had been sent for me by the Taye Diggs look-alike. As we pulled away from the town home, Si-Si waved good-bye.

The driver pulled up to the Palazzo Venezia in minutes. To my surprise, it was empty in front of the museum. I expected crowds of cultured, well-to-do people. But just a few cars were parked along the front of the building, and what looked like a few members of the press.

I stepped out of the car with the help of the driver, who had gotten out to open my door for me. Immediately, I was approached by my date.

"I can take it from here," he said to the driver, his voice heavy with an accent that didn't sound Italian. He tipped the driver and sent him on his way. Then he turned to me and with a gleaming white smile said, "Celess, I'm Cliff. It's nice to meet you."

I smiled back and said, "The pleasure is all mine."

Right then I felt very comfortable with the well-dressed, small-framed, good-looking, chocolate man. Si-Si had nothing to worry about, I thought, and neither did I. The vibe I got from Cliff was cool.

"Let's go inside, shall we?"

We got to the front door, which was manned with two guards. Cliff showed the guards some kind of badge, and they let us in. We walked through the large open museum and went straight to the exhibit. It was just the two of us.

"Are you the only person in Rome interested in seeing art by Sebastiano del Piombo?" I asked jokingly, as I read the name of the artist from the brief bio beneath the painting. "Where is everybody? This is open to the public, right?"

"Well, not until tomorrow," he explained.

"Ohhhh," I said. "So you get special privileges, huh?"

He smiled and said, "I'm a collector, so I tend to be invited to these exhibits before the general public."

"Must be nice," I said.

He started to give me some background on the artist and his paintings, and I was actually interested. My date had gotten off to a good start so much so that when Cliff offered to take me out to eat afterward, I didn't hesitate.

We walked outside and over to his champagne-colored Lexus LS 600h L hybrid, which was parked directly in front of the museum. Cliff was a perfect gentleman, opening my door and assisting me in the passenger's seat.

The car reeked of brand-new leather, and I wondered if he had bought it right before coming to the exhibit. It wouldn't have surprised me.

He put a destination in his navigation system, and we were off. The ride to the restaurant, which was one I had heard of and kept meaning to try but never got around to it, was spent with Cliff asking me a lot of questions about myself, my likes and dislikes, birthplace and date, and occasionally complimenting me on my beauty and fashion sense. We conversed the whole time, causing me to forget all about calling Si-Si and reporting my whereabouts.

We pulled up to the Supperclub tucked on a side street, Via de' Nari. Once inside the famous spot, it was easy to see why *Condé Nast Traveler* had named it the best Italian restaurant in the world. The stunning interior was a fusion of classical and contemporary. There was even a glass panel in the floor that looked down onto an original well.

We were taken into a room called La Salle Baroque, and we removed our shoes and climbed on the big bed, where we would be served our four-course meal. That was my first taste of the oh-so-talked-about Roman banquet.

As we lay back on white pillows, our servers, whose faces were painted ultraviolet, brought out silver platters of food and wine. The DJ played upbeat lounge music, and videos were projected onto the walls.

Our fellow patrons were all extremely fashionable, and they received their food at the same time as we did. An entertainer performed while we ate meats like baked calf's heart and Dover sole from the fixed menu.

As if the experience wasn't engaging enough, massages were given for a small fee. I must say, I was impressed by the Supperclub and by Cliff for choosing to take me there.

"That was so good," I said to Cliff once we left the unique dining experience.

"It was," he agreed.

"Was that your first time eating there?"

"That was my first time at that particular one, but I have been to the one in Amsterdam on numerous occasions," he answered.

"You're well traveled, I see. That's cute."

"Cute, huh?"

"Yeah, cute. I like a man who has been some places."

"Well, what about yourself?" he asked. "Besides here and your hometown in America, where else have you been?"

"A few places," I responded. "Most recently, though, South Africa."

His face lit up. "I'm from South Africa."

"Oh, really?" I wasn't as surprised as I sounded. "That explains the accent. I knew it couldn't have been Italian."

"Nooo. I haven't been here long enough to adopt their

tongue." He chuckled. "What part of South Africa did you visit?"

"Cape Town."

He nodded. "Beautiful place."

Just then Cliff's car pulled up in front of us. He swapped places with the valet attendant as I got into the passenger's seat.

"I know I'm supposed to have you back, but I have a room at the Excelsior. I'd love it if you could spend the night with me. I'll pay for the extra time."

I was buzzed from the wine and cocktails I had guzzled at the Supperclub, and I was having fun with Cliff, so going back to his hotel was an invitation I was willing to accept.

"That could work," I said softly.

We reached the hotel, and nothing short of amazing was the luxurious home away from home at which stayed many celebrities, statesmen, and artists who visited the Eternal City. Once in Cliff's suite, I got comfortable. I placed my pocketbook, which had my phone in it, down on the couch. On top of it I placed my mink stole.

"So, Cliff," I started, as I looked out the window at the zipping traffic, "just how long have you been residing in Florence, Italy?"

When I turned and looked at him, waiting for his answer, Cliff was hanging up my stole and pocketbook.

"Since my wife passed seven months ago," he said.

"Oh, wow, I'm sorry to hear that," I told him sincerely.

"Thanks," he said, walking from the closet to the minibar. Grabbing a bottle of red wine, he asked if I wanted a drink.

"Sure," I said, walking over to him.

I stood beside him. He picked up a wineglass, and both

our eyes landed on a small bag of what appeared to be cocaine that had been hidden under the glass.

He got nervous immediately as he tried to divert my attention from the bag.

"Let's go have a seat on the couch, why don't we?" He took the wine and glass and walked across the room.

I hesitated, glancing at the bag once more, then I followed him to the couch and took a seat.

He was getting ready to sit down with me when I asked him, "Was that what I think it was?"

"What?" He was a terrible actor.

I smiled at his attempt to pretend like he didn't know what I was talking about.

"It's okay," I told him. "If it was, I just wanna know if I can have some."

"Are you sure? I mean, I'm so sorry that it wasn't in a better hiding place. I just didn't intend to have company tonight."

I got up and stood in front of Cliff. He was tense. I wrapped my arms around his neck, resting my elbows on his broad shoulders. I started kissing him softly and slowly, allowing him to ease up. When he finally did, I asked him again.

"Can I have some?"

"Is it because you really want it or because you're just trying to make me feel better about having it?" he asked. "I don't want you to acquire any habits on account of me."

"Trust me, you won't be giving me anything that I haven't had before," I assured him.

"Okay," he said, slipping out of my arms and walking back over to the minibar.

He retrieved the lonesome bag of cocaine and handed it to me. As I held it in my hands, a feeling of excitement came over me. I felt my adrenaline kick up a notch. Then my intuitive voice started speaking to me, reminding me that I had been clean for months and that I shouldn't regress. I was listening to myself and started to tell Cliff never mind, but by that time he already had the mirror, razor blade, and a couple of straws on the table ready for us to party.

Just this once, I told my internal voice. I'll go back to being clean tomorrow.

I joined Cliff as he snorted a line. We took turns. When we were finished with the bag, we both wanted more. Cliff made a phone call, and, like room service, it was brought to the door. That time, instead of a small nickel bag, Cliff had a whole eight ball.

We laughed and kissed and fondled each other between doing lines of the coke. By the end of the eight ball we were butt naked and fucking like two strays in heat.

Cliff's dick was as big as his bank account and as good as his product. I felt like I was in love with the man. He instantly became my new BFF. Florence was about to be seeing a whole lot of me. If only that was a good thing.

March 2008

"Hap-py birthday to ya, hap-py birthday to ya, haaap-py birthday! Haaaap-pyyyyy birth-daay, hap-py birth-day . . ." We all sang the Stevie Wonder rendition of "Happy Birthday" to Si-Si, who seemed to be more attentive to who was singing than to why they were singing.

Her eyes kept scanning the small crowd of guests whom Andrew and I had invited to her surprise twenty-fifth birthday party.

"Still no word from Ryan?" she whispered over her shoulder.

"Nope. Andrew been calling his cell and his office. No answer at either one," I told her.

"That's strange. It's like he just fell off the face of the earth," she said, describing Ryan's disappearance after he left to go back to New York over a week ago. "I'm worried," she continued.

I patted her shoulder. "He's cool, I'm sure. Maybe he had a shitload of work to handle when he got back. You know how it is sometimes when you go away and leave your business in somebody else's hands. You come back to problems and shit that weren't there before you left."

Si-Si nodded, but it didn't seem like she really felt me. Instead, she was in a daze. She walked away from the circle of friends and associates and vanished inside the rented villa on Lake Como.

I told everyone that they could help themselves to any one of the twenty-five different flavored cakes. They wasted no time either. Meanwhile, I ran in the villa behind Si-Si.

"What's wrong, Si-Si?" I asked, walking briskly behind her as she walked through the villa, peeking her head in and out of the various rooms as she passed them.

"Something. I just don't know what yet," she said, serious concern in her tone.

I let out a sigh. "I'm telling you he's either working hard or playing hard. I'm sure it's nothing for you to be worried about. Just like a few weeks back when you were scared to death when I went on that date with Cliff and didn't call you to tell you I was staying the night with him. You swore up and down something had happened to me. And look, I was just having a ball. Ryan is probably doing the same."

The sixth room Si-Si peeked in was the one. She went inside. I followed. She headed straight to the computer that was sitting on the oversize wooden executive desk. She turned it on and waited while it booted up.

"What are you doing?" I asked her. "You gonna send him an e-mail?"

"I'm just checking the headlines," she said, quickly tapping away at the keys.

I crossed the room and positioned myself behind Si-Si. She was scrolling down the Google news page, skimming over headlines. Nothing stood out. She started her search over, but this time, instead of typing Ryan's name in the search box, she typed in "Emperor's Club VIP." The page re-loaded, and a list of options popped up. Skimming through the search results, both Si-Si and I noticed a lot of headlines about the club being in the middle of a sex scandal involving New York's governor, Eliot Spitzer.

Si-Si opened one of the links. It was a full-fledged article that the *New York Times* had posted about a prostitution ring being run out of the New York–based escort agency, the Emperor's Club VIP. Both Si-Si's and my mouths dropped wide open. Si-Si's instincts were correct. Something had gone wrong.

"Shit," she said, reading the article. "They shut the club down and arrested motherfuckas."

"Oh, my God. Ryan," I thought aloud.

"Go get Andrew," Si-Si said, her eyes stuck to the computer monitor.

I left the room that looked more like a public library than a room inside a house and walked back out to the terrace to get Andrew. He was mingling with friends when I approached him.

"Excuse me. I hate to be rude, but Andrew, may I talk to you for a minute?"

Andrew gestured for his friend to give him a second. Then he followed me into the house. I led him to Si-Si.

"We have a problem," she said the minute Andrew walked through the door.

"What's the matter?" Andrew asked, walking over to her.

"The Emperor's Club has been shut down. The governor of New York was dating one of their girls, and it caught up with him. They say he spent about eighty grand—"

"On who?" I blurted out.

"I don't know. But it was over some time. Anyway, the feds have traced the money back to the offshore account and everything. I think we need to close our account and cut all ties to the club, like asap," Si-Si spoke with urgency.

Andrew listened intently, and his whole demeanor changed. He had been bubbly and relaxed, enjoying the beautiful weather, food, and drinks, but now he looked as if he had seen a ghost. He stiffened, almost terrified.

"I say we go now." I broke the silence. "It's no telling what steps they've already made in investigating the club further. They could be on our heels right now, for all we know."

"I agree," Si-Si said. "They already mentioned my name in one of the articles," she confessed.

"What?" I was shocked. That could mean that we were too late. They were probably getting arrest warrants for us as we spoke. That sent me into a panic. I was not trying to lose my freedom.

"It just said that the Web site had girls named Sienna and Christine," she explained, making light of the fact that her name was brought up in the press.

"All right," Andrew finally said. "Let's go. We have to close up the accounts, shut down the site, and change the business name." He turned to leave the room, and after Si-Si shut down the computer we followed him.

"Did any of the articles mention Ryan?" Andrew asked as we walked down the hall.

"No. Not one," Si-Si replied.

"I hope he isn't cooperatin'," Andrew mumbled.

"He wouldn't," Si-Si said strongly.

We had to interrupt the party and let our guests know that an emergency had popped up and that we would have to end the festivities early.

Right away, Andrew called our Web site developer and

told him to take our site down. Meanwhile, Si-Si called all the girls who were currently on dates and instructed everyone to end them. She let the customers know they would be refunded their money. I had to call Marco and let him know not to allow any of his club's patrons access to any of our girls. At first, I didn't want to tell Marco. I thought it would be a bad idea to ruffle his feathers, but Andrew assured me that it would be worse for us to go without telling him and have him find things out on his own. I understood that and went along with his and Si-Si's idea to give him the heads-up.

"Hey, Marco, it's Celess," I said when he answered his phone.

"Hey, Celess, how's it going?"

"Not good." I cut to the chase.

"What's going on?" His demeanor changed.

"You may have heard, but the agency in the states was busted by the feds. So even though they may not know anything about our connection to them, we're taking precautions and shutting everything down right now," I explained.

"Really?"

"Yeah, so don't bother booking any more girls."

"Wow. So does that mean you won't be using my space anymore?"

"Pretty much. I mean, we're gonna stop everything right now."

"Well, where are you guys going to pick up and move to? I mean, we can keep things running, just on a quieter level, down low, you know what I mean? I doubt the U.S. situation will have any effect on us over here in Europe."

"Yeah. Maybe not, but we don't want to take any chances, especially not with your name on the line."

"Well, I mean, we were doing so well. I'd love to keep you

guys as partners. I mean, I really don't foresee some cops from America putting their noses in our business over here."

"Well, you can't be too sure,' I said, wondering why Marco was pressing the issue of our remaining in business with him. It was he who made the speech about taking his freedom and reputation seriously. He should be thanking me for giving him the heads-up and saying good-bye, I thought. "Well, why don't you all think about it for a couple days and then get back with me?"

"I don't think that's going to happen," I stressed. "We're closing everything—accounts, everything," I reiterated.

By then Andrew and Si-Si were looking at me with What-is-he-saying? expressions.

"But thank you for everything, Marco. And um, Andrew will give you a call a little later." I repeated to him the message Andrew had mumbled to me.

"All right," Marco sang, as if I was making a big mistake.

I hung up the phone.

"He was trying to get us to keep operating," I told Si-Si and Andrew.

"And he was trying hard too, apparently," Si-Si said.

"Unusually so," Andrew added.

"Well, despite what he thinks we should do, that's a done deal," Si-Si said.

It took us about an hour to stop all operations. Andrew was even able to close our accounts from his computer. His being high up in banking worked in our favor. We were allowed access around the clock. Business hours didn't apply to us.

After everything was disabled and terminated, the three of us went to the town home, picked up Lisha, and then we all went to Andrew's villa.

It seemed as though the night took forever to turn into day. Si-Si and I could hardly sleep. Between thinking about Ryan, hoping he was okay, and praying that we wouldn't be detected, we were tossing and turning the whole night. It was about six in the morning when we both finally fell into a deep sleep. And just minutes later, Lisha's cell phone rang loudly, waking us right back up.

We watched her intently as she picked the phone up off the chest of drawers that was in the huge guest room Si-Si, Lisha, and I shared.

"Hello?" she answered, her voice sounding puzzled.

We watched Lisha like a hawk, examining her facial expressions for clues about who was calling at such an early hour.

"Ryan?" she asked, relieved. "It's Ryan," she said to us.

Si-Si jumped up and reached out for the phone. Lisha handed it over.

"Where are you?" Si-Si asked, not wasting any time. "Okay, come to the second house." Then she hung up.

"What did he say?" I was curious.

"He just landed at the airport," she said.

"He's coming here?"

"Yeah."

"Did he say anything about what happened? Or if everything was okay or not?"

"Well, when I asked him where he was he said, 'I just landed at Leonardo da Vinci,' then he said, 'I'm safe,'" Si-Si said. "So I take it he got away cool. But I guess we'll see when he gets here."

At that moment there was a tap on the bedroom door.

"Come in," Si-Si said.

Andrew opened the door slowly. His curly head was the

first thing we saw. Once he saw we were all awake, he walked into the room.

"Who was that?" he asked, nodding toward the phone.

"It was Ryan," Si-Si said. "He's on his way here from the airport."

"What did he say?"

"Not much over the phone, except that he was safe."

"You think he's being followed at all? Why would you tell him to come here? What if he's trying to set us up?" Andrew appeared to be panicking.

"I know Ryan. He's loyal, almost to a fault. He would drown before he would jump from a sinking ship, and he damn sure wouldn't sink it himself," Si-Si replied.

"I hope you're right," Andrew said, still uneasy.

About forty minutes passed, and then the doorbell rang. Andrew went to look at the security monitors. He saw a taxicab drive away from Ryan, who was standing outside Andrew's gate with a woman we didn't recognize. Andrew was hesitant about buzzing him in.

"Who is that with you?" Andrew spoke through the intercom.

"A friend of a friend," Ryan answered vaguely. "Take my word, she's cool."

Si-Si nodded to Andrew to let Ryan and the Jane Doe in. For whatever reasons, Si-Si clearly trusted her brother.

The minute he walked through the door, we bombarded him. That was after a round of hugs, of course.

"What the hell?" Si-Si started it off.

Ryan was shaking his head. "I know. I know. It's crazy, right?"

"Crazy is not the word," Si-Si said. "You have to explain everything to us, starting with your friend of a friend."

"Naja, could you go in the other room, please?" Ryan

asked the buttermilk-skinned, curly-haired girl whose baby face was riddled with grown woman scars.

She got up, giving each of us the eye, then walked into the kitchen.

We sat down on Andrew's custom chenille sectional. Ryan had the floor.

"Let me start at the beginning," he said.

"Please do," Si-Si encouraged, still carrying attitude in her tone.

"When I went back home a week and a half ago, you know, to check on things, make sure everything was running smoothly, I got a call from my homey, Antione. He was one of the first people I met in New York back in '04 when I got there. He was the one who actually helped me start the club. 'Cause him and his girlfriend had a little house they ran girls out of. Anyway, we remained cool over the years, and he called me asking for a favor. He wanted me to buy her," he nodded his head toward the kitchen, referencing the girl. "He needed money so he was liquidating."

"And you said yes?" Si-Si asked, not looking for an answer. "That was the part of this business we were supposed to leave out. Remember? Only willing bodies."

"I know. But he was in a bind, and if I didn't buy her, someone else would. And knowing this trade, she could have ended up in worse places than with me. Plus, somebody took me in when I had no one, and if it weren't for that, I probably would have been dead before my eighteenth birthday. You know that, Sienna."

Si-Si rolled her eyes, but she didn't dispute the claim. "So okay, you bought her, then what? When did you find out that a governor got busted for soliciting one of your top girls?"

"Right after I got done with her situation," Ryan pointed to the girl. "Ain't that some shit."

"Well, how did you get out? We read that they arrested four of the starting players," Andrew asked, addressing his number one concern.

"I wasn't around when it all went down. Thank God, I had got the call from Antione about the girl, 'cause I was with him when the feds showed up at the office."

"So they didn't look for you or anything? I mean, there's no warrants out for your arrest?"

"Unless one of my partners snitched on me, they won't. They don't know me. I've never put my name on anything. I learned that from Chatman. The only way the feds would have been able to get me is if they caught me in the act, like they did my old boss. But like I said, I wasn't at the office at all. I heard about everything from the papers and the news. Just like y'all did."

"So why the hell it took you over a week to contact us and get back here?" Si-Si questioned.

"She didn't have any ID or nothing," Ryan explained, referencing the girl again. "I had to drive all the way to Philly to hook up with my man Sammy—"

"Sammy who?" Si-Si cut him off.

"Sammy, document Sammy. You know Sammy."

Si-Si's jaw dropped. "You're still in touch with Sammy?"

I cut in, "What part of Philly is he from?" I wondered if I too knew Sammy.

"He's not from Philly," Si-Si answered me. "He's from Florida. He worked with our boss back in the day. He used to make up IDs, passports, and Social Security cards, everything so we could get girls in the country," Si-Si said, breaking it down.

"Yeah," Ryan continued. "I hooked back up with him, like,

a year after the convictions. He was working for an accounting firm in New York, and when I was looking for an accountant, I stumbled across his name online. I set up a meeting with him, and when I walked in and seen him sitting there, I was like, damn," Ryan reminisced.

Andrew, Lisha, and I were just watching Ryan and Si-Si, our eyes going back and forth between the two like we were watching a Ping-Pong game.

"Oh, my God. That's crazy." Si-Si's attitude began to lighten up. "So what is he doin' in Philly now?"

"He left the firm and started working independently. He got a client out Philly who supposed to be a big-time dealer—a kingpin."

"What's his name?" I asked Ryan. I knew most of the dealers, especially big-timers.

"I don't even remember. I think it was something like Courtland, though," Ryan said.

"Oh, Kenny," I said. "I know who you talkin' about. His name was ringing right when I left for L.A."

Ryan nodded. "Yeah, that's it, Kenny." Then he continued, "But anyway, I had to wait for Sammy to get me the documents for her before I could board a plane out here," Ryan said. "I wanted to call, but I wanted to wait until I actually got out here first. That way I wouldn't have to do too much talking on the phone, plus, getting through airport security would let me know whether or not I was cleared, and I didn't want to call y'all before I knew that and take the chance of leading the feds to y'all," Ryan explained, proving the loyalty Si-Si credited him with all along.

"So now what?" Andrew asked. "What do we do?"

"Shut everything down," Ryan suggested.

"We already did," Si-Si said.

"Well, that's all we can do for now," he said. "Just lay low until this blows over. I still don't know if my name is goin' come up in the interrogation room or not. So I'm just goin' hide out for a while."

Andrew shot Ryan a worrisome look.

"Not here, though," Ryan said. "I got enough money to rent something for the time being."

Andrew was relieved. "Not that I wouldn't help you out," Andrew said. "I just have a lot more at stake than you all. I have a lot more to lose."

"Andrew, we know, trust us," Si-Si said. "None of us wanna take a fall, but I think I speak for us all when I say you would be the last person we'd want to see go down. We understand you're our lifeline. So we put your safety first."

"Well, it's sure as hell good to know that I'm dealing with a smart group of people," Andrew said.

We ended our talks and gathered our things to disperse. Si-Si, Lisha, and I were all going back to the town home. Ryan was going to stay at a hotel—at least until the morning, when he could scout out a flat to rent.

"Can she go with y'all?" Ryan asked Si-Si and me as we were getting into the limo outside Andrew's house. "I don't want her to get stuck running around with me."

Si-Si looked at me. I didn't know what to say. I mean, the girl looked rather young. Could we get charged with kidnapping if we got caught with her? And I didn't quite understand the buying and selling of girls yet. That shit sounded like a crime to me. It was bad enough we were possibly in hot water as it was. I, personally, didn't think we needed any more shit on the bottom of our shoes.

"What you think?" Si-Si asked.

"Can't she just go back to the States? Where's her family? She's a juvenile, isn't she?"

The girl stepped toward us, and with a pitiful face she looked both Si-Si and me in our eyes.

"Yes, I'm a juvenile, but I don't have a family. My mother had my older brother killed in a robbery. Then, two years later, she killed my older sister. She stuck a needle filled with heroin in her chest. I'm her third child, which means if I go back I would be next. Please, I beg you, take me with you. I will work. I will clean. I will cook. I will dance. I will do anything. Just take me with you," the girl pleaded.

I had actually shed a tear, and though Si-Si didn't cry, her glassy eyes indicated that she wanted to. How could we say no to that? Maybe Ryan was right. Maybe the poor girl was better off with us.

"Fuck it," Si-Si said. "Come on."

We parted ways with Ryan, got in the limo, and headed back to the center of Rome.

It had been a week and a half since the news broke of the Emperor's Club being exposed and shut down, and since then we shortened our business name to the Roman Empire. We used Naja and Lisha to open new bank accounts with fake names using false IDs and documents that we were able to get from Sammy. And last but not least, we stopped using the Diva Futura Channel Club as our meet-up venue. We didn't want to risk dragging Marco through the dirt. Between Si-Si and me, we had enough enemies.

Business picked up right where it had left off. Most of our customers were unaware of or uninterested in what went down in America. They continued booking dates. In the meantime, Andrew had withdrawn a little from the business. He still had a great deal of money in it, but he was less active—partly because he was dealing with a lot of business issues pertaining to the faltering economy back home. Apparently, many of the high-paid CEOs and Wall Street bankers were going under, and the government was being called upon to bail them out. All of the drama had been concerning him a great deal, being that he had a stake in the Federal Reserve.

Ryan, on the other hand, became much more active. Our agency was his only means of income now that the New York branch had gotten shut down. He had said on numerous occasions that it was meant for him and Si-Si to link back up the way they did and at the time that they did. He figured that if he had never come to Rome, he would have been working at the New York office nonstop like he had before he got that unexpected call from Si-Si. He had no doubts that he would have been taken to jail right along with his partners.

He had gotten an apartment in Piazza Navona, not too far from the town home Andrew had lent us. It wasn't as big as ours, but it was just as luxurious. He had stopped coming over to our house as much, often busy working from his own house. But secretly, Lisha and I had made a couple trips over there to revisit the night of passion we shared in Cape Town.

One night at the end of the month, Si-Si suggested we all go out to dinner. Andrew was back in town, and she thought we could all use a stress reliever. She reserved a table at the rooftop restaurant at Hotel Raphael near Ryan's apartment.

We all were there, Andrew, Ryan, Lisha, Naja, Si-Si, and me. I even invited Cliff, whom I had been talking to since our date the month before. He fit right in too, and everybody was nice to him.

We were eating our meals and drinking our drinks when Ryan asked us for our attention. We stopped what we were doing, and all our eyes fell upon him. He swallowed his food and cleared his throat. Then he began, "I just wanna say that I am so happy that I'm here right now with y'all. Most of y'all don't know, but I been through a lot in my life, and it seems like through everything, it's been one person steadily keeping me out of trouble . . ." Ryan looked at Si-Si, and with tears forming in his eyes, he continued, "Sienna, thank you for saving me once again. I haven't gotten the chance to tell you how grateful I am for what you did for me in Miami, for you risking yourself to make sure I would walk free. That was the most a person ever did for me in my entire life. Not even my mom would do that for me. I never told you, but I wound up finding my mom. It took me about seven months, but I found her. And when I did, when I walked in that little shack she called a house in Dade County, just twenty miles from where she knew I lived, I ran up to her and grabbed her so tight I thought her tiny bones would break. And you know what she did?" The tears finally broke free. "She said, 'Ryan, son, get out of here before you get me killed?'"

At that Si-Si broke down with Ryan. She got up from her seat and walked across to cradle him in her arms. He sobbed like I had never seen a grown man do before.

"She didn't say, How have you been? I missed you, I love you. None of that. She just told me to go. To run away. To leave before Chatman showed up to kill her."

"That's no fault to your mother, Ryan. Chatman probably put death in front of her so vividly that her fear of him overpowered her love for you. Don't hold that against her," Si-Si tried to console Ryan.

"But I've seen Chatman put that same fear in you, and you didn't let it overpower your love for me . . ."

Si-Si didn't say anything. She just rubbed Ryan's head. And after a brief silence Ryan said, "You are my guardian angel, and I just wanna let you knows I appreciate you for that."

Si-Si bent over and kissed Ryan on the top of his head. He squeezed her tight before letting her go and excusing himself to go to the bathroom. I passed Si-Si my unused napkin. And Andrew followed my lead by asking the waitress to bring us more napkins. Everybody was in tears. It was one of the most heartfelt moments I had witnessed between two people. The bond that they showed they had when they hugged the first time Ryan met back up with Si-Si was explained that night over dinner. And it was clear to me that Si-Si and her brother had some deep, deep feelings for each other. They had been through some stuff together, and whatever it was it made their love for each other stronger than the love between any two people I had ever known or could imagine. I prayed for them that night, that they would both survive their pasts and happily grow old together. I had no idea that in just a few weeks I would be praying for just the opposite.

April 2008

The sun was shining extra bright. Flowers looked noticeably vibrant. The wind blew a light, comfortable breeze. It was the epitome of a beautiful spring day. I had plans on getting out and enjoying it, but while I was in the shower, I got an unexpected visitor.

Bzzzz . . . Bzzzz . . . Bzzz.

Who the hell was that at the door, ringing the buzzer like they were crazy, I wondered.

Bzzz . . . Bzzz . . . Bzzz. The ringing persisted.

I turned off the water and got out the shower, grabbing the white terry robe that was hanging on the hook on the back of the bathroom door and throwing it over my dripping body. Meanwhile, the buzzer was still ringing. I jogged down the flight of stairs, picking my cell phone up off my dresser on my way out my room. Dialing Si-Si, I nervously pep-walked to the front door.

Bzzz . . . Bzzz . . . Bzzz.

"Who is it?!" I yelled as I got close to the door. I looked through the peephole and saw nobody but Ryan.

I opened the door relieved.

"Boy!" I screamed at him. "You had me thinkin' you was the muthafuckin' police!"

"Celess, who's here?" Ryan asked in a panic.

"Just me, why?" My nervousness returned.

Ryan then barged past me. He walked into the living room, rubbing his head.

"Ryan, what the hell is the matter?" I walked behind him, following him in circles as he paced the living room.

"You sure ain't nobody here?" Ryan double-checked, paranoid. "Where's Naja? Where's Lisha?"

"Si-Si took them to their doctor's appointment," I explained. "Why? What's wrong?"

"Celess, them pussies gave me up. Them fuckin' faggots ratted me out!" Ryan raged.

"What do you mean? Who ratted you out? What is goin' on?"

"My partners at the club. I went to my apartment today, and my mafuckin' door was kicked in! Shit was everywhere! Then the lady across the hall said a bunch of detectives were there lookin' for me!" Ryan explained, beads of sweat gathering on his forehead.

I walked over to Ryan to try to get him to stand still for a second. He was making me dizzy and scared. I couldn't think. I needed him to calm down.

"Ryan," I began, wrapping my arms around his waist, "just take a minute to breathe," I told him. "It's not the end of the world. Just 'cause them mafuckas snitched don't mean shit. The cops ain't got you yet. Plus, you don't even know for sure if it was the damn cops. Somebody could've robbed ya apartment. I'm sure that shit happens in Italy too."

"Naw, naw." He wasn't convinced. "Why would my neighbor say the cops was looking for me if it was just a robbery? She specifically said *polizia*."

"She probably was scared as shit after seeing niggas kick ya door in. She swallowed the first shit they fed her ass," I tried to rationalize my theory.

"Naw." He still wasn't seeing things my way. Then he broke away from me and walked over to the couch. He stood in front of it for a moment while he bit his thumbnail and gathered his thoughts. Then he sat down on the edge.

"She said detectives came here looking for you."

"Did they leave a warrant?" I asked him.

He looked up at me. He shook his head. "I don't know. How would I know?"

"It would've been somewhere visible. I mean, don't get me wrong, I don't know exactly how shit works over here. But back home, they leave a warrant after they been in a nigga's house. They want you to see that they were there and that they had a right to be there, and on top of that, they want you to know that they got ya ass," I explained, recalling a story Tina's ex, Khalil, told her about one of the times the cops kicked his door in. That pussy, I thought immediately after the brief memory of Khalil, the guy who shot me and killed my best friend, played in my mind.

Ryan rubbed his chin. Then he seemed to be calming down some. I walked over to him and sat beside him. I put my arm around his shoulders and pulled his head close to my chest.

"Don't jump to conclusions. That'll make you panic, and panicking will run your ass right into danger," I said comfortingly. Ever since Ryan's emotional meltdown at the restaurant a few weeks ago, I'd been extrasensitive when it came to him. I felt the need to console him, to be there for him and offer healing.

I rubbed his head, going in the same direction of the flow of his soft, black waves. Then I worked my hand down to his shoulders and upper arms, tracing his defined muscles with my finger.

He lifted his head up a little and poked his lips out.

"Are you asking me for a kiss?"

He didn't answer. Instead, he poked his lips out some more.

I leaned in and gently pressed my lips against his.

"Everything'll be all right," I told him. "As soon as Si-Si gets back we'll figure out what to do."

He used his tongue to part my lips as he started kissing me passionately. All the while his hands made their way through the opening of my robe and started massaging my breasts. In no time I was lying on the couch, my legs spread apart, with Ryan between them pouring all of his emotions into me.

I was so into the sex that I didn't even hear the key turning in the door. Furthermore, I didn't hear the three pairs of footsteps from the front door to the living room. It wasn't until I heard "Ryan!" that I opened my eyes.

"Si-Si!" I yelled, jumping up from beneath Ryan. I grabbed my robe and clenched it together at the middle, trying to conceal my naked body.

Meanwhile, Ryan leaped to his feet and was haphazardly buckling his pants.

It was obvious we were both extremely embarrassed. We had not only been caught by Si-Si, but we had been caught in front of Naja, who looked frightened, and Lisha, who looked like she wanted to crack up laughing.

"I thought I made it clear to y'all," Si-Si said, a look of disgust in her eyes.

"My bad," Ryan was short on words.

"Ya bad?" Si-Si questioned. "Is that all you can say to me?"

"Well, what do you want me to say?" Ryan asked.

Si-Si huffed. "I specifically told you on not one, not two, but three different occasions not to do it, Ryan!" she stressed. "And you just dismissed me and went ahead and did it anyway? In my house, on my couch?" she said dramatically, her disgust turning to anger.

"Si-Si," I tried to butt in. I never seen her so mad before, and while I couldn't understand why Ryan and me fuckin' had her so upset, I should have respected her wishes.

"Celess, please." She shut me down.

Ryan smirked. "I know what you told me, but why?" he finally asked of her reasoning. "What does it matter that we fucked? Me and you aren't together. And we haven't been since you went on a fuckin' mission and found out we were related," Ryan said, as if he had become angry too.

Si-Si stared a dagger into Ryan. Then before she spoke, she turned to Naja and Lisha, whose mouths were on the floor.

"Give us a minute," she said softly.

Without hesitation, they disappeared from the living room. I wanted to be excused myself, but then again I wanted to hear that shit. It sounded to me like Ryan and Si-Si had more than sibling love for each other. It was sounding like some incest shit had gone on between them. And if so, that would explain Si-Si's strong intent to keep us from going there with each other.

Si-Si turned back to Ryan. "You act like you're mad about

something. Like I wanted us to be related or something. Like that was my excuse to leave you alone."

"Well, that's what you acted like," Ryan said. "You seemed like you were happy to find out all that shit. Like you was looking for a reason to part ways. Shit, you had the annulment papers signed and everything. You wasted no time. You didn't even try to confirm shit. You just left me, just like that. Now, you get jealous 'cause I'm fuckin' ya friend?" Ryan laid out Si-Si's cards.

"Jealous?" Si-Si decided to address that issue first. "If it was a jealousy thing, I would've tried to keep you from fuckin' all the girls you had in ya bed since we been back in contact. This has *nothing* to do with me being jealous!"

"You sure about that?" Ryan asked, cocky.

"I'm positive! In fact, dumb ass, I didn't want you fuckin' Celess because I was lookin' out for you! Just like I was lookin' out for you when I got those annulment papers and I left you! But you've always been naïve, so I can see why you would think me tellin' you not to fuck Celess was 'cause I was jealous! You would think that!" Si-Si turned to walk away.

Ryan reached out and grabbed her arm. "Then what was it, Sienna? Huh? How were you lookin' out for me this time?"

Si-Si turned around, looking like she wanted to say something, but instead she ground her teeth and shook her head.

I myself wanted to intervene, apologize for going against Si-Si's requests and calm the situation. But having found out that the two of them had had a relationship and were married and everything, I lost my train of thought. I totally forgot that the argument was about Ryan and me, and my focus switched solely to Si-Si and Ryan's past affair. So much so that I never stopped to think about why, if not jealousy, Si-Si was so enraged that Ryan and I had sex.

"Yeah, that's what I thought," Ryan said. Then he mumbled, "If you wanted to look out for a nigga, you should've let me bust my nut."

Si-Si's head whipped around like she needed an exorcist. Her eyes were on fire. "I was tryin' to save ya ass from fuckin' a man!" she said, spite flying off her tongue.

"What?!"

"*Si-Si!*" I yelled at her.

I got up from the couch and started to walk out the room. Ryan got hold of my robe as I passed him.

"What did she say?" he asked me.

"Let 'er go," Si-Si said. "It's not her fault you wanted to prove a point to me."

"You a man?" Ryan asked me, ignoring Si-Si's command to let me go.

I didn't say anything, but the crazy thing was, I wanted to. I wanted to say, Fuck no! Si-Si trippin'. But I couldn't. It was like a cat had my tongue for real.

"Let her go, Ryan! You should've put ya fuckin' pride on mute and listened to me."

"That's why you ain't want me to . . . 'cause she a man?"

"Si-Si, get ya brother!" I finally found my voice.

At that, Ryan let go of my robe, but only so that his hands could be free for him to wrap around my neck.

"Ryan!" Si-Si shouted at him.

"What, you like one of them fuckin' transsexuals or something?" he asked me, pain in his eyes.

Once again, I couldn't talk, but this time it was because I wasn't getting oxygen. Ryan had my neck in his hands so tight it felt like my head was going to pop off.

Si-Si ran over to him and started trying to pry his hands off me. He ended up using his muscular upper body to bump the shit out of her. She stumbled backward, and in the short seconds it took for her to gain back her composure and try again to get Ryan off me, he had snapped and was striking me in my face with his balled fist. By the time Si-Si managed to stop him, both he and I were covered in blood. My blood.

My face felt numb. I could hardly see anything from the tears and blood that poured from my eyes. Holding on to my blood-plastered robe and barely able to stand, I was screaming at the top of my lungs, *"Fuck you, Ryan! You can't hurt me! Nigga, I been shot in my face at close range with a mu-fuckin' thirty-eight caliber! And you think you did something? You ain't do shit! Nigga, fuck you!"*

Ryan could have used my taunts as fuel to keep whipping my ass, but Si-Si said something to him that must have hit a nerve.

"What, you think you Chatman now?" she yelled as he was coming back toward me. "You done turned into the man who beat ya mother like that to the point where she denying her only son? You're that guy now?"

Ryan stopped in his tracks. He turned to Si-Si. I should have been relieved, but I was more fearful. I thought Ryan was going to pound on Si-Si and finish us both off.

"Fuck you, bitch!" he said as he brushed past her and stormed out the front door.

As soon as he left, Si-Si ran to the door. It sounded like she was putting the top lock on it. I managed to make my way to the stairs. I held on to the banister, using it to hold me up as I headed up to my room, where I washed my face.

I was throwing on some clothes when Naja entered.

"Oh, my God, are you okay?" She gasped, holding her hands over her mouth.

"I'm fine," I said. "Go on."

"You sure, Celess?"

Then Lisha appeared. "Celess!" Her South African accent expressed deep concern.

"I'm fine!" I stressed.

"No, you're not," Lisha said.

"I'm alive, ain't I?" I told her. "Now leave me alone."

Then in walked Si-Si carrying a freezer bag full of ice cubes in one hand and a wet towel in the other.

"Celess, where are you going?" she asked me, obviously noticing I was filling up a duffel bag with clothes.

"None of ya business," I told her. As far as I was concerned, she was lucky I wasn't whippin' on her ass. She damn sure better not say shit else to me, and she better not get in my way when I go to walk out the door, I thought.

"Celess, don't do this," she said. "You need to put this ice on ya face before it swells."

I zipped the duffel and threw it over my shoulder. I walked a few steps to the doorway, where Si-Si was standing.

"Si-Si, I suggest you get the fuck out my way! If my face do swell, what the fuck do you care? You're the reason it happened! So move before I move you, and I'm fuckin' serious," I stated fiercely.

I was so mad I started crying all over again. I really was in fighting mode, and I knew in my heart that if she didn't move out of my way, I was liable to kill that girl.

"I'm sorry," she said. "I swear I didn't want it to come out. But he—"

"*Move!*" I yelled with all the might my windpipes could muster. If there was any glass in the room, it would've broken for sure.

Si-Si stood frozen for a second, then she moved to the side and let me pass. Though that didn't stop her from begging me not to leave. She followed me down the steps and into the garage. Even Naja and Lisha were begging me to stay. I ignored them, got in the Mercedes S65 AMG that I had bought myself with my first big check from the agency, and sped off.

Once out of the garage and onto the busy streets of Rome's center city, I fiddled around my purse for my cell phone. I went to dial Cliff and noticed my last call was made to Si-Si and lasted thirty-two minutes. The thing was, I never spoke to Si-Si. I called her just as I was about to answer the door to see if she was expecting anybody. But I thought I'd hung up after I'd realized it was Ryan ringing the bell. Shit, I thought. I must have forgot to end the call. She must have heard everything Ryan and I was talking about, and that was probably why she had gotten home quicker than she should have. She rushed home on account of Ryan's drama and wound up catching us doing the one thing she asked us both not to. Fuck, I thought.

As the guilt for my actions sunk in, I proceeded to dial Cliff.

"Hello," he answered on the first ring. He sounded happy.

"Hey, baby," I tried to sound sexy through my tears.

"Hey to you, sexy," he said.

"You wanna party?" I asked.

"Always," he said.

"You got any neve?"

"Snow?" he quizzed. "Why do you want snow on a beautiful day like this?"

"Because when everybody is goin' left, I wanna be goin' right," I said, still trying to maintain my sexy.

He chuckled. "Well, in that case," he said, "I think I can make it snow on a spring day."

"Good. I'm on my way to the train station. I'll call you when I board to let you know what time to pick me up from Santa Maria Novella Station."

"Okay, beautiful. Have a safe ride."

"Thank you. I can't wait to see you."

"Me too," Cliff said.

"Bye."

"Ciao."

I zipped through the narrow and crowded streets as best I could, anxious to get to the Termini Station. I needed a quick fix more than anything, and to know Cliff had me covered was satisfying. I couldn't get to that nigga fast enough.

Dear God, I began to pray silently in my head, please see to it that I get to Cliff's safely. And please see to it that Ryan and Si-Si forgive . . . matter fact, fuck that nigga Ryan and that bitch Si-Si. I hope they both get what they got comin'.

May 2008

Cliff had been overprotective of me since I showed up at his house in Florence looking like I had just stepped out of a boxing ring. He screened my calls and barely let me out of his sight, fearing I would be sweet-talked into going back to Rome. Though I had no intention of doing that, at least not at first. I had been well taken care of, fed fine dishes, clothed in whatever I wanted, and supplied with all the coke I could ask for on demand. So I felt no need to go back.

But then as the days turned into weeks, and the weeks turned into a month, life with Cliff changed rapidly as his money depleted. We went from eating all three meals out every day and shopping for clothes, instead of washing the ones I had, to ordering in and taking my clothes to the dry cleaner. The partying we had been doing four nights a week dropped to only Friday and Saturday nights.

I didn't trip about the downsizing right away. I mean, I understood Cliff when he said we needed to slow down, especially when he made me aware of the fact that we had run through eighty grand in a matter of weeks. But I had no idea that it would get as bad as it did.

Ding dong! ding dong!

"That must be the pizza," Cliff said as he got up off the couch and walked to the door.

I was crouched up on the sofa watching an Italian game show, well, looking at it, I guess I would say, because I really wasn't watching it.

Cliff opened the door and gave the delivery guy his credit card. The delivery guy ran it through a handheld machine and waited a few seconds.

"*Mi dispiace—*" the delivery guy started.

Cliff cut him off quick. "English, please."

The delivery guy translated, "Sorry sir, it's declined."

My face wrinkled as I wondered how a man as wealthy as Cliff could have a credit card that didn't have 22 euros on it.

"Declined?" Cliff acted surprised. "Try this one," he said, pulling another card from his wallet.

The delivery guy repeated the steps from the first card. A few seconds went by, and he again reported to Cliff that his second card was denied.

At that point Cliff turned to me. "Celess, do you have some money for this food?" he asked me.

I was hungry as hell, and the fresh Italian pizza smelled good. But I would be going against everything I stood for if I paid the tab. And not because I was against a woman paying, but because of how it came to be. It wasn't like I had offered. This man was asking me, and out of desperation at that. He was broke. Too broke to pay for a damn pizza. How that could be was beyond me. And I had to get to the bottom of it before I spent a dime on that nigga.

"Cliff, are you serious?" I asked him. "You don't have any money at all?"

"I thought I had some money left on my card." Cliff shook his head. "I have to call my bank. I'm sure I have something."

I was still confused. "What do you mean, you're sure you have something? Aren't you rich?" I asked, in front of the delivery guy and all. I didn't care. I needed to know his true financial status. I couldn't be fuckin' around with him, dissin' Si-Si and Ryan, who were tied to my source of income, if he was cracked. That wasn't about to happen.

"Must we talk about this now?" he snapped, clearly embarrassed. "Can you just loan the money so he can go?"

It took me a minute to respond, as I was tempted to snap back on his ass. But I figured I would spare him any more embarrassment. I stood up and walked over to the door. Handing the guy a 50-euro bill, I took the box of pizza and the grapefruit soda.

The guy placed the credit card swipe machine under his arm while he dug in his pocket to get my change.

"Keep it," I instructed him, looking Cliff in his eyes. I needed him to see how shit was supposed to been done from the start.

"*Grazie millie,*" the guy said, a big grin on his face as he left.

Cliff reached out to relive me of the pizza and soda, but I moved aside and took the items into the kitchen myself. That nigga wasn't touchin' my shit until he explained to me what was going on.

"Cliff, what is your money issue? I mean, I understand if you tell me we can't continue to blow through eighty grand like it's smoke, but between two credit cards, you mean to tell me you ain't got twenty-two banknotes? How do you expect me to stay with you?"

"I will check my account in the morning. There's some mistake, I'm sure," he said, flustered, as if he didn't want to talk about the subject.

"I don't think you understand." I was not lettin' him off that easy. "I'm just goin' make this as clear as possible. Are you or are you not rich?"

Cliff hesitated. His eyes wandered in every direction but mine. "I'm not rich." He threw up his hands.

"Then where the hell did you get all that money you blew on me? What the fuck, was you a lottery winner or some shit?"

He sighed and said, "I had money from my wife's life insurance policy," his voice cracking toward the end of the sentence.

"Are you kidding me?" I asked. "So you're broke then? This whole thing was a façade? Unbelievable. How long did you expect it to last like this? Did you really think I would move in with you like you suggested? I mean, how did you plan to take care of me? What were you thinking?"

"I wasn't," he blurted out. "I was just having fun! Finally getting over the pain of losing my wife. I just wanted to forget it, to escape my reality for a while, that's all."

"So basically you had me on a joy ride?"

Cliff didn't say anything, and in his moment of silence I kindly left the kitchen, went upstairs to the master bedroom, and packed my bags. I was going back to Rome, to reclaim my security. Even though I wasn't quite over the shady shit Si-Si did and the sucker shit Ryan did, I couldn't let how I felt interfere with my livelihood. Money over bitches, I mumbled to myself as I threw my clothes, new and old, in my duffel.

I helped myself to the leftover line of cocaine that was still on the mirror from the night before. Brushing my nose off, I took a last glance in the mirror to make sure I didn't have any residue in or around my nostrils. Then I grabbed my cell phone off the dresser, threw it in my pocketbook, then left the room.

I walked down the steps, and Cliff's bum ass was sitting on the couch eating a slice of the pizza he couldn't afford.

I wanted to cuss him out so bad, but I figured I'd let him live. He had just lost his wife, and although he had misled me, I understood he was grieving.

Seeing me packed, he put the pizza down and stood up from the couch.

"You're leaving me?" he guessed.

"Sorry, Cliff," I said to him as I walked past him toward the front door. He followed me.

"Sorry for what? I'm the one who was wrong. I shouldn't have told you to come move in with me knowing I couldn't support you for long. I shouldn't have jammed you up like that," he admitted. "What do you have to be sorry for?"

"Sorry for your loss," I told him.

With a cracked smile on his face and tears in his eyes, he said, "Thank you." He kissed me on my cheek and thanked me again. "Are you going to be all right?" he asked.

I nodded. "It always turns out that way," I told him.

"Will you call me some time just to let me know you're safe?"

I shrugged my shoulders. "Why not," I said.

I was so over Cliff. He had me so annoyed with him. I mean, why would he string me along all the way until he got down to his last dime? One day we're eating, and the next day we're not? What did he expect, for *me* to start supporting us? What a way to bring me down off my high. Oh, my God, I was pissed. But I was trying to be nice for the sake of his sanity. I knew one thing, though, from that point on, I was not taking a nigga's word or flash for shit. Before I even thought about becoming dependent upon a man, I needed to see proof of income. I'd be damned if my next prince turned out to be a frog. Fuck that.

I took a cab to the train station and caught the train for the two-hour ride back to Rome. I wanted to call Si-Si and let her know I was coming, but since I didn't bother charging it, my phone been dead for days. I couldn't even check my voice mail.

I grew anxious as I arrived at my destination. The sun was starting to descend behind the clouds. Once I got off the train, I walked to the parking garage rather quickly—partly due to my anxiety and partly due to the darkness descending. I jumped in my car, looked around the front and back seats just to make sure no one was in there and that everything was intact the way I'd left it over a month ago. I had become very cautious since the whole ordeal back home that sent Si-Si and me flying to Europe in the first place.

Everything was as I left it. I started the ignition, put the car in drive, and backed out my parking space. I paid the hefty fee and exited the garage onto Rome's dark city streets. Zipping through the moderate traffic, in minutes I was parking at the town home I shared with Si-Si.

I hesitated in the car for a while before I actually went inside the house. I practiced what I would say to her when I first seen her. I would simply tell her that I was sorry, just like I knew she was sorry, and after taking time away to clear my head, I wanted nothing more than to move forward. I was sure she would agree and that would be that.

I walked up to the door, leaving my duffel in the car. I didn't feel like carrying it out. I just wanted to get in the house, face Si-Si, and then get in my bed and rest my head on my own pillows.

I stuck my key in the lock, but before I could turn it all the way, the door flew open. Si-Si gripped me up and wrapped her arms around me so tight. Immediately behind her was Andrew. I got a chance to look at him while Si-Si was hugging me. And I didn't know how to read his face as it expressed both relief and sorrow. I knew the heavy emotions couldn't have been just for me. I knew in my gut that something else besides the fact that I was back home had caused their reactions to seeing me. I just didn't quite know what it was. Nor did I think I wanted to.

June 2008

*I*t had been two weeks since Ryan's funeral, and Si-Si was still stuck in her bed, buried in her sheets. She hadn't spoken about his death or anything after she initially told me the story the night I returned from my monthlong living arrangement with Cliff. I'd never forget that night either. I'd walked into the house planning to squash our beef and was greeted with the terrible news that Ryan had been found dead in his apartment only three nights before I showed up back at the town home. Police called it suicide—said he shot himself in the head.

Si-Si was just plain gone after that. She blamed herself. She thought that her calling him Chatman and bringing up his mom while he was already angry about finding out about me, on top of the fact that he was fearful his partners had ratted him, were the straws that broke the camel's back. Whenever I would try to talk to her about the tragedy, she would just say, "I wish I could rewind the time. I would have never said those things to him."

I didn't believe that Si-Si drove Ryan to kill himself. In fact, I thought maybe it was my fault. Maybe his coming to grips with the fact that he had been carrying on a sexual relationship with me, a former man, made him do it. The only reason I was able to get out of bed and not sleep my days away like Si-Si was because of my dependency on cocaine. I was again hooked on the first and only illegal drug I had ever taken in my life. Every day, for most of the day, I was taking time and money to devote to my habit. I used the same dealer Cliff had called to his hotel the first night I had met him and saw the bag of powder at his minibar. The dealer made himself available whenever I needed him. I had gotten to the point where I was spending a grand a day with him. And not that I was smoking that much in one day. I was stashing some just in case anything happened to him and I wouldn't be able to get it on the spot.

A lot of shit changed after Ryan's death. Lisha got back on a plane to South Africa, and Naja, the poor lost girl, went with her. As for me, I was high most of the time, not really giving myself a chance to feel what was happening around me.

Meanwhile, the escort service was being run by Andrew. I couldn't tell you how many clients we had or how much money we were bringing in. All I knew was that for the past thirty days my personal bank account showed daily deposits of 5,000 euros. Si-Si's, I imagined, showed the same, as did Andrew's and Ryan's, until he passed. So when I added that shit up, I concluded that the Roman Empire was doing pretty damn good. I kept telling myself I would sit down with Andrew one day to get all the details about the business so that I could be caught up. But every day I woke up I found myself more interested in getting high than doing anything else.

I was in my room listening to archived editions of Jamie Foxx's satellite radio show online. I was laughing hard at the Superhead interview when Andrew walked in.

"Celess, you and Si-Si get dressed. I want you two to take a ride with me," he said.

"Where to?" I asked.

"The set of a movie I invested in," he said, as he disappeared from my doorway.

I sprang up. That sounded like a plan. I would like to go on the set of a foreign film, I thought. Plus, it beat sitting in the house all day. I went in Si-Si's room and jumped on her bed. She was curled up in a fetal position, sound asleep.

"Si-Si, wake up," I announced. "We 'bout to get you out this house!"

Si-Si cracked open her eyes as if it hurt. She took one look at me and then pulled the covers over her face.

"Si-Si!" I shouted. "Come on now. Enough is enough." I plopped down on her bed beside her. I cuddled her in my arms and whispered in her ear, "You need to get out this bed. You'll feel so much better."

She nudged away from me, moaning and groaning in the process. "I don't want to, Celess. Please . . ." she whined.

"Andrew wants us to go down on the set of a movie he got money in. Don't you wanna see what it's like when they shoot foreign films?"

"Not really," she moped.

"Si-Si, what, you goin' sleep the rest of ya life away?"

"If I can," she said.

"Do you think Ryan would want that?" I was trying everything to get her to change her mind.

"It ain't like I ever did what Ryan wanted me to do before," she said. "Just let me be. I'm not ready to go out nowhere. Seriously, Celess. I'm hurting too bad." She began to cry.

I felt her pain and figured I would allow her to grieve the way she saw fit. I'd been in that position before, and no matter what anyone said or did, I didn't come up out it until I was good and ready. And my shrink, Ms. Carol, had tried hard too. But I didn't budge. I needed to heal in my own time.

"All right." I sighed, getting up off her bed. "I'll at least bring you some food back."

I walked out of Si-Si's room and shut her door behind me. Then I got dressed. It was scorching hot outside, so I threw on a multicolor Pucci sundress and a pair of gold Pucci flip-flops. On my way out the door, I grabbed my pair of gold Dior sunglasses off my jewelry chest, put them over my eyes, and met Andrew in the garage.

"No Si-Si, huh?" he asked, upon my getting in the passenger's seat of the Ferrari.

I shook my head.

He twisted his lips, huffed, then, after a brief pause, put the sports car in drive. We did nearly a hundred miles per hour the whole way to Piazza Sant' Agostino Square.

We pulled up to the Angelica Library next to the church of Sant' Agostino. Judging by the light package alone, it was a big-budget film we had rolled up on. There were people everywhere. Streets were blocked off, including the area we were pulling into. One of the police officers who was directing traffic stopped us as we got close to the barrier. He stated the obvious—that no one was allowed to enter without a permit. Andrew explained to the cop who he was and assured him he would only be a second. The cop eased up but told him to leave the car running in case he needed to move it before we returned. Andrew agreed, and the cop allowed us to pass through. I was impressed. They had shit set up like a Hollywood studio production was going down. And I'd be damned if it was.

The minute we got out of the car, one of the producers approached Andrew.

"Andy," he said, giving him a nickname. "What's up, buddy?"

"What's up, Brian?" Andrew replied. "Brian, this is a friend of mine, Celess. Celess, this is Brian, a producer on this film."

I smiled and shook the guy's hand. After the introduction, the guy led us over through a crowd of people, PAs, camera crew, lighting guys, extras, etc. straight to the director. It was then that I realized it wasn't a foreign film, titled *Obelisk* like the slate read, being shot there but an American one. I was on the set of the next movie by the *Da Vinci Code* author, *Angels & Demons*. Now, had that been before I moved to Italy, I would have been ecstatic to meet and connect with the director, Ron Howard, but at that time, while I was possibly wanted for murder, running into Ron or any Americans in the film business was the *last* thing I wanted to do.

I tried to think of a way to make my escape before Ron and I came to face-to-face, but he peeped from behind the Panavision camera way too fast.

"Ron, this here is my guy, Andy. The one I was telling you about. Looking to do more things beyond this," Brian said, putting Andrew and Ron in touch.

"A pleasure to meet you," Andrew said, then he immediately introduced me.

"Ron, this is one of my business partners, Celess. She's

done movies before. You may already know her." He picked the wrong time to boast.

Ron smiled as he reached out to shake my hand. Then, as quick as lightning strikes, his smile turned upside down.

"Celess?" he quizzed, a troubling look on his face. "Oh, my God, it's you."

He snatched his headphones off and stood up from the director's chair, almost stumbling. I was scared stiff, and although I wanted to run, my legs wouldn't allow for it.

"You're the one. You're the one they keep talking about on Nancy Grace. They're looking for you, for that murder in L.A. a few months ago," he said, blowing my cover.

Andrew laughed. I guess he figured there was no way in hell Ron could have been serious. He thought he had to be joking. But I was sure he got the picture when finally my legs cooperated with my mind, and I took off. I flew back past the PAs, camera crew, lighting guys, extras, and everybody else. Thank God I had decided to wear flats.

I ran out to Andrew's car, remembering it had been left running. I jumped in the driver's seat, threw the gear in reverse, and slammed my foot on the gas pedal. The tires screeched when I came then to a sudden stop. Putting the car in drive and again slamming down on the gas, I sped away from the library like a bat out of hell, driving straight through the wooden barrier that was up to keep traffic from entering the location and ignoring the commands to stop from Andrew, Ron, two police officers, and whoever else.

I did a hundred miles per hour back to the town home because I needed to get home as fast as humanly possible. I jumped out the car so fast, I almost forgot to put it in park. I ran up the steps, taking two at a time, and once I reached the top, I started pressing the buzzer and jamming my key in the door simultaneously. Whichever would get the door opened first, I thought.

My key won out, and I burst through the door. By that time, Si-Si was standing at the top of the stairs looking confused. I guessed she was on her way to answer the buzzing doorbell.

"Celess, what the hell?" she complained.

"Si-Si, we gotta get the fuck up outta here now!" I told her with extreme urgency as I ran up the stairs in her direction.

"Whyyyy?" she whined. "What happened?"

"I don't have time to explain, but long story short, Andrew took me to the set of an American movie. Ron Howard recognized me and told Andrew I was wanted for murder."

I started throwing any and everything of Si-Si's in a piece of luggage that I tossed in the middle of her bed. Once I felt like I couldn't get any more items inside the suitcase, I stopped. I closed it and had to practically sit on top of it to zip it shut. I dragged it to the floor and rolled it over to Si-Si.

"Take this and go get in my car," I instructed her as I turned off my ever-ringing cell phone. Then I left her room and darted to mine.

I packed myself a suitcase too and rushed out of the room. Instead of her being in the car where she was supposed to be, Si-Si was still standing at the doorway of her bedroom holding the suitcase handle looking dazed.

"Si-Si!" I screamed at her. "Let's go!"

She snapped to attention and followed me out the house.

We ran to the garage and to my car, which was parked next to Si-Si's Range Rover Supercharged.

"What about my car?" she asked.

"We gotta leave it!" I told her.

I opened the trunk of my car and tossed my suitcase inside. Si-Si followed my lead. We both got in the front, and I swiftly maneuvered the car out of its parking space and out of the garage.

"Where are we gonna go?" Si-Si asked, her frail body shrunk down into the passenger's seat.

"We goin' have to leave the country," I said, thinking of one thing and one thing only: protecting my freedom.

Si-Si—in three-day-old pajamas, a sloppy ponytail, and a pair of footies—resembled an escaped mental patient as she lay back in the seat, strangely silent and looking out the window at the world as if it were her first time doing so.

She seemed like she had given up, like nothing mattered to her anymore, not even the fact that our time evading the law was about to be up. And it was no doubt in my mind that, had I let her, she would have thrown in the towel. And for a brief moment, I had to question if it would be worth taking her with me. I mean, her head was no longer in the game, and she was bound to slow me down. I fought with the decision as I drove toward the airport. Then, as I pulled up to the curb at ticketing/check-in, I was forced to make a decision.

I put the car in park and turned to Si-Si. "We need to split up," I blurted.

"What?" she asked, and not because she didn't hear me either.

I looked away from her, bouncing my eyes back and forth between the side and rearview mirrors.

"It's the best thing to do for us both," I bullshitted. "They're lookin' for two girls, not one. We'll have a better chance of slipping through if we're on our own."

Si-Si was quiet, but her face read so much confusion and hurt.

"Plus, you need to go to a hotel and clean yourself up. You can't expect to get on a plane looking like that. You'll draw all the wrong attention to yourself and be busted for sure," I said, throwing in some truth.

Si-Si nodded, staring out in front of her at nothing in particular. She mumbled, "I guess you're right."

At that I told her to take my car to a nearby hotel and get herself together. I put a few hundred euros in her palm and kissed her on the cheek.

"Meet me in Cape Town at the Table Bay," I told her. "I love you," I added.

A tear dropped from Si-Si's eye as she sat frozen in the passenger's seat. I got out and retrieved my luggage from the trunk. I walked around the car to the passenger's-side window and reminded Si-Si of the instructions I had just given her.

"Si-Si, you have to go now," I told her.

She snapped into action and climbed from the passenger's seat to the driver's seat. I waved good-bye to her as she slowly drove away from the curb.

Trying my hardest not to cry, I walked over to the ticket counter. I bought a one-way ticket to Cape Town and checked my luggage.

Paranoia surrounded me as I passed through security, walked to my gate, and boarded my flight. Even in the air, I was still looking over my shoulder. I had never felt such fear in my life. And to make matters worse, I was worried about Si-Si. She was probably somewhere in cuffs, thanks to me. I had failed her, and the realization of that hit me like a ton of bricks. I fucked up big time for that. I was supposed to have ridden it out to the end with her. I wasn't supposed to turn my back on her like I did. I was dead wrong, and my conscience was making me pay. In an attempt to right my wrongs, I prayed for Si-Si's safety, and while I was at it, I prayed that my conscience and not karma was the only thing I had to worry about.

July 2008

I had spent the first six days in Cape Town drinking and partying, the next six days snorting coke, and if I had used the following six days to be as self-destructive, I would have let the devil win. I needed to pull myself up out the rut I had been in and get back on my job. But the truth of the matter was, I hadn't stopped feeling shitty about leaving Si-Si in Rome on her own, especially in the state she was in. The drinking and the drugs took my mind off that fact, and so I indulged to avoid thinking about her.

But my time was valuable, and I was wasting it. So I told myself that, come the first of the month, I would start to regroup. I needed to check my finances and use whatever I had left to get a place to stay. Then I needed to look for work. No, not a nine-to-five, but a rich old man with rich old friends. I figured I could start up the Roman Empire down there in South Africa. Shit, it was the only business I knew that required only a Web site, a bank account, and some bad bitches. I could get those three in my sleep.

The first day of the month rolled around, and instead of sleeping until three in the afternoon, I got up at seven A.M. I was ready to carry out my plan. The first person I reached out to was Lisha, whose cell phone was off.

Then I called Naja. Same story. Goodness, I thought, those two hoes together can't afford a phone line?

I looked around my room for a phone book and couldn't find one. I called the front desk and after the clerk apologized several times for my inconvenience, she said she would send one up. I didn't feel like waiting so I went downstairs and grabbed the White Pages from the hotel lobby, took it back to my room, and scanned the list according to Lisha's last name, De Lange. I dialed everyone listed under the surname. After about the fifth call, I decided to give up. Not because I was tired or anything, but because one of the names that was listed gave me a different idea.

I was going to call Cliff. He was from South Africa, and although he wasn't rich like I had thought he was, he knew how to walk the walk and talk the talk. He had to have gotten that shit from somewhere. I was sure he had one rich friend, and if not, he could at least point me in the right direction.

"Celesss," he sang into the phone.

"No need for me to ask if you're happy to hear from me," I said.

"Of course I'm happy to hear from you. I never thought I would again," he told me.

"Well, neither did I, to be honest with you," I admitted. "But life has a habit of bringing me to do things that I never thought I would."

"Yeah, like what?" he asked.

"Well, for starters," I began, "I'm in your neck of the woods."

"Florence?" he guessed incorrectly.

"No. Your original neck of the woods. And"—I cut him off before he could say my location over the phone—"before you say anything more, I want you to go out and get a prepaid phone. Call me on this number after you do."

"Okay." He was confused but smart enough not to ask any questions.

"And Cliff," I said before hanging up, "don't make me wait too long."

I hung up with Cliff and called the toll-free number on the back of my debit card, then followed the prompts to speak to a customer service representative.

"Hello, thanks for calling Trillion Stars. How may I assist you?"

"Hi, I'm calling to get the balance on my account."

"Okay, I'll be happy to get that for you. May I have your account number, please?"

"One second," I said, digging through my Louis bag for my checkbook. I opened it up and recited the numbers that were on the bottom of the checks to the woman on the phone.

"Please verify the last four digits of your Social Security number."

I turned the checkbook over and read the woman the four digits that were scribbled on the back of the checkbook. It was from the made up Social Security number we had provided when opening the account.

"Who am I speaking with today?"

"Charlotte Baxter." I read the name that was written right beneath the four digits.

"Okay, Ms. Baxter, thanks for verifying that information for me. Your balance as of today is sixty-three thousand four hundred fifty euros."

"Okay," I said, doing a bit of light math in my head. The last I had checked we had about 59,000 euros in there, and that was about two days before the fiasco on the *Angels & Demons* set. I wondered who had deposited more money in the account since then and why. I had actually expected the account to be empty, or at least damn near. I thought that would have been the first thing Andrew would do once he found out why Si-Si and I had really come to Italy.

"Can you tell me what the last transaction was?"

"Sure." The woman obeyed my every command. "It looks like a deposit in the amount of four thousand fifty euros was made on June 27."

"All right." I had enough information. "Thank you."

The woman asked if there was anything else she could help me with, and when I responded no, we ended the call.

So Andrew was still booking dates, I figured. And he was having the money go straight to our account too. That was strange. But good news for me, nevertheless. I wrote out a series of nine checks all in the amount of 7,000 euros. I left the "pay to the order of" line blank, still unsure who I would get to cash them. I put them all in an envelope and sealed it. Then I put the envelope in my pocketbook.

I left my hotel room and headed down to the lobby to return the phone book. I stepped off the elevator and almost had a heart attack. Si-Si was at the front desk of the Table Bay hotel, apparently checking in.

I wanted to scream her name, but that wouldn't have been smart, particularly because I was sure she was checking in under a false identity. I just held my excitement in until I got up behind her.

"Give me one minute to get the keys to your suite." The tall, slender, dark-skinned woman excused herself just before disappearing into one of the offices behind the counter.

Right then, I tapped Si-Si on her shoulder, and when she turned around, I brought her into me and squeezed her so tight. She returned the hug, and then we let each other go. She looked me over as I did her. And the girl looked good—different, but good. She had certainly bounced back from the depressed state I had left her in. And even managed not only to clean herself up but to take on a whole different look.

Tears gathered in my eyes as I sang, "You made it!"

She nodded with a huge smile on her face.

"How? And why did it take you so long? I was scared to death that something had happened to you," I whispered, expressing my concerns a little bit late.

"Well, thanks to Sammy," she mumbled, placing her hand on the chest of the man who stood beside her. "I was able to get docs to get on the plane . . ."

"So this is the infamous Sammy," I said, putting a face to the name I had heard from both Ryan and Si-Si.

"Nice to finally meet you." He shook my hand.

Then Si-Si continued, "I had to wait for the alert of us being spotted in Rome to die down. They had the airports on lock just waiting for us to show up there. You lucky you made it out before the police put the word out."

"That explains your disguise," I said, referencing Si-Si's shorter, darker hair. "You look like Victoria Beckham now."

At that she pulled out a driver's license and handed it to me.

"Vida Beckham," she said, smiling, reciting the exact name that appeared on the ID.

"I'ma have to get one of these," I said, handing her back her new identity.

"Yeah, right away," she agreed.

I hugged Si-Si again. I was so happy that she was there and was all right. Then, when the front desk clerk returned, we decided to finish our conversation up in the room. Si-Si got her keys from the woman, and she, Sammy, and I took the elevator up.

"What's the phone book for?" Si-Si asked of the White Pages, which I had forgotten was tucked under my arm.

"Oh shit," I said. "I was supposed to leave this at the front desk. Seeing you threw me right off."

"Who were you lookin' for anyway?" she asked.

"Oh, Lisha and Naja," I answered her. "I'm tryin' to start the business up down here."

"With those two?" she quizzed.

"Not necessarily with them," I clarified. "But I was thinking about employing them."

"Well, did you find them?"

"No."

"Well, keep lookin' 'cause we definitely settin' up something out there." Si-Si was on the same page as me. "That's why I brought Sammy down here with me. He's going to help us do this thing right. Where it'll be untraceable."

"That's what's up," I chimed in, glancing over at Sammy.

The *ding* from the elevator put our discussion on pause. We stepped out of the elevator and proceeded to walk down the hall to Si-Si and Sammy's room.

"His client back in Philly got jammed up on a murder

charge, so he's looking for something new to throw some money at that'll throw twice as much back at 'im," Si-Si explained.

My cellphone and Sammy's rang at the same time.

He stepped to the side to answer his. I looked at mine and saw that it was Andrew. I let it go to voice mail like I had each and every time he had called since I had run off on him. I would have gotten rid of my phone if I hadn't wanted to ensure Si-Si had a way to reach me if she needed to. But now that she was back, I planned to dump the phone.

"Leah, Leah, you don't have to do all that." Sammy's whining brought my attention to his phone conversation. "No, no, no, that won't be necessary. Just be at my office next Thursday at three. I'll meet you there with a cashier's check."

"There goes your investment dollars, huh?" Si-Si asked the minute Sammy got off his call. Apparently I wasn't the only one listening in on him.

"Not all of it," Sammy said. "That was my client's girlfriend. She doesn't know exactly how much money of his I have. I'll give her enough to shut her up, then invest in your thing with the rest."

"How much are we talkin'?" Si-Si asked.

"I can probably get away with about a million."

"That'll work," Si-Si said. "Go ahead back to Philly and work that out. Then soon as you get back down here, we goin' structure this thing top to bottom. And we goin' do it the old-school way too. I'm tryin' to take this thing worldwide and build an empire like Chatman did. Only smarter," she dreamed aloud.

I was all in as I listened to her. And it was like hearing the Si-Si I first met. She was back and with a vengeance.

Her focus, her attitude, and her game plan were on point, and I wanted so bad to be right there with her, but somehow I couldn't shake the phony vibes I detected between us. However, I forced myself to ignore the strange feeling that burned inside me and concentrated on being happy that I had my best friend back.

August 2008

"Congratulations, Celess. You are now Bella Cruz," Sammy said, handing me an ID, passport, Social Security card, and even a credit card.

"Vida Beckham and Bella Cruz," Si-Si said. "We sound like wannabes."

"No," I corrected her, smiling, "we sound like boss bitches."

"And I like the sound of that," Cliff said, offering his opinion rather flirtatiously.

"They do sound hot," Naja added her two cents.

"Yeah," Lisha agreed.

"Okay," Si-Si gave in. "If y'all say so." She sighed as she stepped out the pool, wrapped the bottom half of her body with a towel, and walked into the dining room.

It felt good that we were all together. I was glad that Cliff had called me back some six weeks ago and agreed to come out here and help us get clients for our business. He was reluctant at first, stating that he had too many memories of his wife in South Africa to come back. But what it boiled down to was, he needed money. And once I got to telling him how much he stood to make, he flew out here on the first thing smoking.

But although he was hesitant, being out here, back home, surrounded by friends and family members, actually seemed to do him some good. Since he'd been back, he hadn't picked up drugs, at least not to my knowledge. And he smiled and laughed more too. Overall, he seemed a lot happier than he had been when I stayed with him for that month in Florence. I was happy for him.

As for Lisha and Naja, it took two and a half weeks, but Si-Si and I finally found them. We wound up having to trace Lisha's last-known cell phone number, which led us to one of her relative's houses. The relative, in turn, led us to Lisha, who was staying in a one-bedroom apartment with Naja and two other friends. Lisha and Naja were so happy to see Si-Si and me they didn't know what to do. Without hesitation, they packed what little belongings they had and left with us. Both of them agreed to work for us, no questions asked. Lisha would be one of our call girls, like she had in the past, and Naja would be our live-in housekeeper. Si-Si and I wouldn't have felt right making her take dates. She was too young. Even Chatman had waited until Si-Si turned sixteen before he sent her out. So technically, Naja had two more years.

But it didn't matter to either of them what they'd be doing, as long as they could be doing it with Si-Si and me. They were desperate, and not so much for basic necessities—they were clearly able to eat, clothe themselves, and keep a roof over their heads. But they were desperate for the lifestyle they had enjoyed for the short time they'd stayed with us back in Rome. And me of all people knew that once you've gotten a taste of the good life, it was hard to get it out of your system. So when we showed up offering that to them once more, they took it hands down.

Four weeks later, we were all sitting around the pool of our five-bedroom, five-bath Helderberg Estate home in Somerset West, about forty minutes from Cape Town. It was a beautiful luxury house with all the bells and whistles, including an indoor pool, sauna, spectacular views of the Indian Ocean and Majestic Mountains, and even an indoor squash court. A friend of Cliff's, who was a prominent real estate agent with a company called Seeff Properties, was able to get us in the house for under a million USD. We couldn't beat it. And being that we planned to make South Africa our home, we jumped on the deal. Besides, if all else failed, it was a good investment property. So much so that Sammy paid half the price in cash just to be able to put the house in his name. Si-Si and I didn't care. We were able to get in the house without coming out of pocket, and what little mortgage was on it would easily be able to be paid off with our business earnings. It was a win/win.

Anyway, it was the last day of the month—the day we designated to do our accounting. We ordered pizza and planned to spend the day inside going over our profits and losses.

"The pizza's here. Are y'all ready to work?" Sammy asked after he had given me my new identity package. And being that he was the only one who knew the real reason Si-Si and I needed new identities in the first place, he made sure whenever he was in front of the others to emphasize the fact that the false documents were made for us so that we would be able to open bank accounts that wouldn't trace back to any of us. Everybody bought it too, especially Lisha and Naja, because they had done that exact thing for us back in Rome.

"I guess we are," I said, getting up from the lounge chair I was stretched out on.

I followed Sammy through the sliding-glass doors that led to the dining room. Lisha and Cliff ended their game of Connect Four and trailed after me. Meanwhile, Naja got out of the pool, dried off, and began cleaning up the empty soda cans, cooler bottles, and whatever else any of us had left out by the pool.

Once in the dining room, Sammy, Si-Si, Cliff, and I all took seats at the table. Shortly after, Naja entered. She went into the kitchen, washed her hands, then began to serve all of us the pizza we had ordered. Lisha took her slice on a paper plate and headed for the stairs.

"I'm going up to take a shower," she said, leaving us to our business dealings.

"I'm right behind you," Naja said, disappearing from the dining room.

"Okay," Sammy began. He opened his laptop, which was already on the table when we sat down. He started punching some keys. Then he proceeded to go through the numbers with us.

"It's been three and a half weeks since we been fully operating with a total of ten girls. And in that time we've booked thirty-five dates. That averages to about three dates a day for four days a week—"

"So you're saying every day of the week we have about seven girls not being booked, and three days out of the week all ten of our girls are not being booked?" Si-Si butted in to clarify.

Sammy nodded. "That's what the numbers show."

"That's crazy," Si-Si said.

"Yeah," I agreed. "We were doing like a hundred times better than that our first week in Rome."

"Wow," Cliff muffled.

"Well, what were you doing in Rome that we're not doing here?" Sammy asked a logical question.

Si-Si took it. "We're doing the exact same thing. The only difference is that our first customer in Rome was a famous soccer player who got busted with our girls by the paparazzi. So we got a lot of free pub," she explained.

"Well, there you have it," Sammy said. "We need to book a date with somebody famous over here. Then alert the press."

"I can put you in touch with a couple famous people out here," Cliff said. "My old fishing buddy owns a management company. He has top athletes, performers, and actors at his disposal."

With a grin on his face, Sammy nodded. "Yes, put us in touch with this guy immediately."

"Wait a minute," I interrupted. "Are you serious, Sammy?"

"Yeah, Sammy." Si-Si had my back. "That could do us more harm than good. I mean, that could get us shut down. We don't know how loose or tight the authorities out here are with this kind of thing yet."

"Plus," I added, "don't forget, me and Si-Si are trying to keep as low a profile as possible."

"I know this. But many times it's the star who gets caught who suffers all the backlash because he's the one everybody knows and cares about."

"Sammy's right," Cliff said. And just then it started to feel like it was a battle of the sexes. "Besides, I have friends in high places. My wife came from a long line of dignitaries. I know the right people we can pay who will keep the authorities at bay."

There was a brief silence as we all nodded and thought to ourselves about the plan of action we were most likely going to take to get our business off the ground. I looked at Si-Si, and our eyes locked. She nodded and said, "That right there will make me feel much more comfortable about pulling that stunt."

"I agree," I said.

"Well, then, let's do it," Sammy encouraged.

"Consider it done," Cliff concluded.

And just like that the four of us developed a system that we planned to use over and over again to launch our escort service not only in South Africa but all over the world. The takeover had officially begun.

It had seemed that Si-Si's and my roller-coaster ride was on its way up again as we were back to living the good life peacefully and free of stress and drama. Our business was quickly becoming one of the fastest-growing escort agencies in the world, with hundreds of clients in numerous countries. We had a total of sixty call girls who were natives in places like Japan and Russia, two of the top five wealthiest countries we had launched in, according to the GDP, or gross domestic product, which Sammy found online. And by being visible in rich areas, we were easily able to target famous and public figures. It was our ability to be linked to the rich and famous that made our agency even more rich and famous. It was the sign of the times. What we had done with our agency was no different than what people like Paris Hilton and Kim Kardashian had done with their careers. And it was genius.

It was time we launched in the Mumbai market, a place we gained knowledge of during the screening of a movie called *Slumdog Millionaire*. It just so happened that Si-Si, Sammy, Cliff, and I had traveled to Toronto, Canada, to scope out business opportunities at the same time the Toronto International Film Festival was being held. We decided to check it out since we were in town. It was a good thing Si-Si and I were in full disguise: Si-Si in her dark, short hair; navy suit; and reading glasses. Me in a China bob wig, big brown shades, and a tan Burberry trench on top of a white tee and jeans. We were dressed so casually and stark, there was no way in hell anyone would recognize us. And the whole time we called each other by our aliases. She was Vida, and I was Bella. But even still, we treaded with caution, staying clear of people like Spike Lee and John Singleton. In fact, we avoided the premiere of Spike Lee's *Miracle at St. Anna* altogether. The chances of one running into not only someone we knew, but someone we knew *well*, were far too great.

So we ended up checking out the screening of a British film about a poor Indian boy who wound up winning $20 million on the Indian version of *Who Wants to be a Millionaire*. It was actually a good movie too, one of my favorites. I never expected it to be so compelling. Neither did Si-Si. She loved it, although she said it reminded her of her relationship with Ryan too much. She couldn't hold back her tears.

Anyhow, the movie gave us the idea to check into India, specifically Mumbai. So as soon as we got back to South Africa, we jumped on it. We figured that once the movie was released to the world, Mumbai would see an increase in tourists and visitors. And we wanted to be right there in position to service them as they flocked in. I mean, most of our business came from travelers who'd rather have a girl waiting in their hotel room for them when they arrived to their destination than spend the time, energy, and money to fly one out with them.

We were at the house setting up shop. Naja was on Craigslist placing ads for workers. Si-Si made it her business to teach that girl how to use the Internet, among other things. She said Naja reminded her a lot of herself when she was younger, desperate for a way out and hungry for the knowledge that would give it to her. For that, Si-Si took Naja under her wing.

Sammy was researching which areas in Mumbai were tourist attractions and destinations, while Cliff was gathering a list of the town's most famous people. Si-Si and Lisha were in the kitchen cooking, and I was busy readying a deck of cards for a game of klawerjas that we planned to play later—a game played like bridge or whist that was as addictive as a damn drug. Once Cliff taught us how to play, it became a twice-a-day habit. That was two weeks ago. Now we were playing it at least after every meal—breakfast, lunch, dinner, and midnight snack. It was sickening, but fun.

Overall, the last three weeks had been nothing but pure fun—full of much needed laughter and playtimes. Si-Si and I finally were able to ease up. We hadn't been as tense. We experienced a freedom and peace of mind in South Africa that we had been missing for so long. Not even when staying with Andrew had we felt we could let our guards down. But somehow, over time, they slowly dropped in the new environment that we felt good about calling home.

"Okay, listen to this and tell me how it sounds," Naja announced.

We all drifted from what we were doing to give Naja the attention she asked for.

"International modeling agency seeks Indian women ages eighteen to thirty who are cultured, well spoken, and outgoing. Must exude sex appeal, be comfortable in the nude, and have an open mind about romance. Enjoy worldwide travel, luxury accommodations, and VIP treatment just for being the beautiful and classy lady that you naturally are. Only serious Cinderellas need apply," Naja read.

Cliff nodded. Sammy looked as if he wanted to say something but couldn't find the words. And Lisha smiled. Si-Si and I glanced at each other, and Si-Si spoke first.

"That shit is better than the one I wrote."

"I was goin' say that," I agreed.

"I like the 'only serious Cinderellas need apply' part," Cliff said.

"Yeah, it plugs the name of the agency too," Sammy added, referring to the Cinderella Service Agency, which was the new name we had given the business since opening it in South Africa.

"Go 'head and post it," Si-Si said. "See what happens."

"Post," Naja said as she tapped a key on the laptop's keyboard.

"Mumbai, here we come, baby!" Si-Si cheered. "We 'bout to be slumdog millionaires our damn selves!"

Si-Si's energy prompted us all to celebrate. We got up from our seats and started slapping one another's hands. We smiled and cheered, boasting of our projected success in a new territory. And in the midst of it all, I was thinking about two things—getting eaten out by Lisha that night and scoring a bag of coke. It was about to be one hell of a night to top off such a productive day, and I couldn't stop smiling thinking about it.

Life is good when it's good, I thought. And I planned to take full advantage of it. Because there was no telling when my luck would turn and the roller coaster would be crashing toward the bottom. And though I knew that day was coming, I didn't know when or by what means. But what I did know was that until that roller coaster tipped, I was goin' to have a mafuckin' ball!

October 2008

*I*t was sweltering hot outside, and the only thing I wanted to be doing was lying up under an air conditioner sucking on ice cubes. But instead, I was on my way out the door to take a flight out to another extremely hot climate: Mumbai, India.

Si-Si and I were going to the country for Lakme, its second fashion week of the year. We figured such an event would be the perfect breeding ground for potential clients and workers alike. I mean, fashion week across the globe was typically attended by the world's Who's Who in business and entertainment. We expected that there'd be gorgeous girls scouting out upcoming trends, men who would eagerly drape them in those trends, and rich men scouting out the hottest models whom they could whisk off the runway for a good time at the show's end. And Si-Si and I would be right there, rubbing elbows, promoting the business, and hopefully booking a few dates, even if it meant booking ourselves. We were down to sell a one-night stand or two. Anything for the progression of the business.

Cliff was going to go with us, but when Sammy got a last-minute call to fly out to Orlando to help set up a business account for his old client who had opened a kid's beauty salon in Disney World, we all thought it'd be best if he stayed home with Lisha and Naja. So it was just going to be Si-Si and me. And I was glad too, because that would give me the opportunity to clear the air with her once and for all.

Since she had come to Cape Town, I had been getting uneasy vibes from her. And it may have been my own guilt or paranoia, but whatever the root of it was, I needed to address it. Otherwise, I wouldn't be able to shake my feelings, and there would be a constant awkwardness between us, despite how hard we both tried to play like it wasn't there.

And that was exactly what we had been doing—pretending everything between us was peachy. I figured our flight to Mumbai would provide the perfect alone time for us both to open up and be one hundred with each other.

"Celess! Let's go!" Si-Si yelled up at me.

"I'm coming now!" I yelled back, scanning my bedroom for anything I might have been leaving behind.

I grabbed my Louis Vuitton Damier suitcase by its handle and wheeled it behind me down the hall and then down the flight of stairs.

"Have a safe flight," Cliff told me as I walked past him standing in the doorway.

"I hope to," I responded, walking to the black SUV that was pulled up in the driveway.

"Let me help you with that," our driver, a medium-height, athletic-built dark chocolate man offered.

He relieved me of my luggage and placed the small rolling suitcase in the trunk of his vehicle.

I thanked him with a smile and then joined Si-Si in the backseat. Our driver, whose physical attributes would have served him better as an exotic dancer than a chauffeur, just situated himself in the driver's seat and backed out of the driveway. By that time Si-Si had already jammed her iPod earbuds in her ears and leaned back against the headrest with her eyes closed. I did the same, listening to T.I.'s latest album, *Paper Trail*, as we made our way to the airport.

We arrived at Cape Town International Airport, and our driver pulled up in front of the terminal for Turkish Airlines. He got out of the car and opened the door for us, then retrieved our bags from the trunk. We each tipped him, then walked inside the busy airport. With it being summer in Cape Town, a lot of tourists were traveling to the country.

Having already checked in online the night before, and not having any bags to check, Si-Si and I headed straight toward our gate. It had been nerve wracking to fly ever since Ron Howard had discovered Si-Si and me in Rome. We hoped for the best but prepared for the worst as we approached the security checkpoint. Trying hard not to look suspicious, I handed my Sammy-made passport and my boarding pass to the petite white woman at the podium who checked travelers' documents before they got to the conveyor belts. My heart pounded in my chest as she examined the passport, making sure the information on it matched the information on my boarding pass and that the picture matched my face. After scanning everything not once but twice, she said, "Bella's a nice name." Then finally she gave me back my documents and let me go.

I was relieved but not for long. It was Si-Si's turn to have her docs examined. Si-Si appeared more confident than I, so I wasn't as worried for her as I had just been for myself.

"Vida," the woman read the name off Si-Si's passport. Then she smiled at both of us and said, "Beautiful life, huh?"

We returned her smile. I remained nervously silent.

"Our mothers were best friends," Si-Si made sense of our fake names.

"Figures," the woman said, handing Si-Si her documents. "Enjoy your trip, ladies."

"Thank you," Si-Si responded with a smile.

I exhaled as we walked away from her. After passing through the metal detectors, I admitted to Si-Si, "I don't think I'll ever get over the fear of going through security at an airport. We'll be eighty years old, and I'll still be paranoid that somebody will recognize us and turn us in to the police."

"Well, shit, by then we'll have lived our lives, so what would it matter?" Si-Si took my statement literal.

"It would matter to me. I don't care how old I get or how much livin' I've done, I want my freedom to the end," I said.

"Yeah, I see, and at all cost, right?" she said with somewhat of an attitude, right before changing the subject. "What gate are we again?" She took out her boarding pass.

"What do you mean by that?" I stayed on topic. After all, I did intend to talk to Si-Si about that whole situation where I abandoned her at the airport in Rome. And her comment presented the opportunity to do so.

"Nothing," she said, trying to brush me off.

"No, tell me," I insisted. "You feel some type of way that I flew out to Cape Town without you and left you to fend for yourself, don't you?" I needed to know.

Si-Si didn't reply right away. But when she did, she replied, "Well, wouldn't you?"

I knew it, I thought. I wished I had brought this up sooner and cleared the air the minute Si-Si showed up at Table Bay. That way we could have been beyond the awkward feelings and tension I had been sensing from her. But it was what it was, and I was not going to cry over spilled milk.

"Yeah, I would," I was honest. "And every second of every day I regretted that. I felt like I shoulda stayed there with you and helped you get yourself together for us to make our escape. And to keep it all the way real with you, I drove myself crazy in those few weeks when I had no idea where you were or what had happened to you. I wished I could have turned back the hands of time. Real rap," I said, finally admitting my wrongdoing to Si-Si.

"Yeah, I know exactly what you mean. I never told you this, but I felt so bad for telling Ryan your secret. I mean, I had warned him not to mess around with you like that, and it was on him that he did anyway. And no offense to you, because you know I love you to death for who you are. But it's just that Ryan was so much more to me than a brother. And I wanted to protect him. I mean, realistically, I knew he wouldn't have wanted to be messin' around with a . . . you know what I'm tryin' to say—"

"I totally understand that," I told Si-Si. "And looking back, I should have been more considerate of that. I wasn't thinking along those lines, and I fucked up."

"It's cool."

"So are we good?" I looked at Si-Si with a half smile. "Have we cut through all the tension?"

Si-Si cracked a smile as well and nodded. We hugged each other tight and officially buried the hatchet.

"All right, now let's tear Mumbai the fuck up!" I said, so much more ready to explore the Indian city now that I felt like I truly had my friend back.

"Let's do it," she agreed as we got to our gate.

For the first couple of hours of our flight, Si-Si and I ordered food and drinks, did some talking, and listened to music. We slept for the remaining eight plus hours. Upon landing at the Chhatrapati Shivaji International Airport, we called Cliff to let him know we had arrived at our destination safely.

"Have fun doing business," he said, cleverly telling us to work and not play while we were out there.

"Sure will," I told him. Then we hung up to make our second call, which was to Sammy.

The phone rang repeatedly until Sammy's voice mail picked up.

"Hey, Sammy, it's Celess. Si-Si and I landed in—"

Si-Si cut me off by shaking of her head.

"Don't say our location over the phone," she whispered.

I took heed and rephrased, "Sammy, we landed safely. Call us when you can to let us know how you're making out. Okay, bye."

I hung up my phone, and Si-Si and I walked toward ground transportation, stopping at a place called Café Coffee Day to get a cup of energy. We had a lot to accomplish in India, and we couldn't let jet lag get in the way of that.

Waiting for us at the baggage claim area was our driver, a tall, thin, golden brown Indian guy. He of course relieved us of our luggage and helped us into his sedan.

"Where to?" the driver asked as he took the sedan out of park.

"Oberoi Hotel at Nariman Point," Si-Si answered, looking at the piece of paper on which she had written our hotel information.

It took us a little under an hour to get from the airport to our luxury high-rise hotel in the heart of the South Mumbai business district. Si-Si and I were tired despite the cups of coffee we'd drunk at the airport, so we planned to go right to sleep, but when the elevator doors opened before us, my eyes landed on someone who changed my plans instantly.

"Michael?" I thought aloud. Then my mind chimed in. No, it can't be, I thought silently. I must be tired as hell, and it's causing my eyes to deceive me, because there's no way in hell I would run into anybody I knew all the way in India, especially not Michael, of all people.

"Celess!" the all-too-familiar voice shouted with excitement and surprise.

I shook my head and blinked repeatedly, trying to get the image out of my sight. I was sure I was hallucinating.

"You know this guy?" Si-Si asked, confirming that what I was seeing was, in fact, real.

I looked at her. She had a confused expression on her face.

"Michael?" I asked again.

"Yeah, it's me," Michael said, waving his hand in front of my eyes.

"Oh, you must be the Michael from Philly?" Si-Si's memory caught up.

"Yeah," Michael verified. "And you're Si-Si, right? From the videos and jewelry campaign ads and stuff?" He sounded like a fan.

Meanwhile, I was watching his every movement, studying every inch of his body. He looked like he had lost some weight, but it was him all right.

"What the hell are you doing out here?" I finally faced facts. "I mean, I never in a million years woulda expected to see you again, and definitely not out here."

"Who you tellin'?" Michael felt the same way. "Never mind not seeing you again, I actually thought you were dead or in jail," he said, his eyes fixated on me.

"Wow," I said. I was at a loss for words.

"That's the picture the news painted," he explained.

"Is it?" I asked, not looking for an answer.

"But here you are live in the flesh. In got damn Mumbai at a five-star hotel. That's Celess for you," he said, "Come here, man." Then he pulled me into a hug.

"O-kay." Si-Si interrupted our holding session. "Celess, I would stay down here with you while y'all play catch-up but I'm exhausted."

"I know. It's cool for you to go up without me. I'll be all right," I told her, figuring I'd skip taking a nap and stay to chat with Michael.

I hadn't seen or spoken to the one-time love of my life since I had left Philly in '07 after the crazy drug-induced disappearing act I pulled on Si-Si and the whole of Hollywood. It was Michael whom I stayed with in Philly for that time period—him and Ms. Carol. And it was during that time that I was able to apologize to him for having hidden my true identity back when we were a couple. We left on good terms, but I never got around to calling him again. Then the unexpected drama occurred, causing me to flee the States and never look back. So that was that.

"I'll take care of her for you," Michael told Si-Si as she stepped onto the elevator.

"All right," Si-Si said, right before she disappeared behind the closing doors.

"Unbelievable," I murmured, looking at Michael.

"Let's sit down," he said, taking my hand and leading me to one of the couches in the lobby.

"So what happened to you, Celess? Where have you been? What have you been doing? I mean, what was all of that drama about on the news? Was any of it true?" He had a sea of questions.

I exhaled and said, "Some true, some false. But to make a long story short, some guy killed Si-Si's mom and then tried to kill Si-Si and me, and we wound up escaping. Then later on we found out that same guy had gotten killed and that the police were looking for us. We got scared and left the country."

"That's crazy!" he exclaimed, but in a low tone. "I remember I was watching TV and they interrupted my show with breaking news about this rising star who had been wanted in connection to a murder in Los Angeles. And then when they said your name and showed your picture, I was like, what the hell," Michael reflected.

I shook my head to erase the memories from that day. "Yeah, I will never forget that, no matter how hard I try," I told him, hinting at the fact that I'd rather not dwell on it.

"But what about you?" I turned the attention to him. "What are you doing out here? I know you're not here for fashion week too."

"Fashion week, huh? That's funny, 'cause I didn't even know it was fashion week."

"I figured that much."

"Yeah . . . I mean, I dress well. I'm in to women who dress well, but . . . I'm no guru or nothing like that," he said, as if I didn't know him already.

"So then what brought you so far from Philadelphia?"

"Well, for starters, I came here from Dallas. I moved out of Philly right after you and I were in touch. I tried to reach out to you to give you my new address and phone number and stuff, but your number was cut off, and when I went by the house of the lady you were staying with, she said you had gone back to L.A. I left her with a letter for you with my information in it, but I guess she never got it to you. Then I saw the news story and was, like, that's it. It's a wrap. I'll never get back in touch with her again."

"So you left Philly and went to Dallas?"

"Yeah, I got a job offer at one of the top architectural firms out there. And that's actually why I'm out here now. My firm got called upon to do a major project here."

"Oh yeah? What project would that be?" I asked him.

"A twenty-seven-story skyscraper . . . and get this, it's a residence."

"What do you mean?" I knew what a residence was, but I didn't register what he was saying.

"This guy, Mukesh Ambani, he's a billionaire—like one of the richest men in the world. He's having a house built: twenty-seven stories, five hundred fifty feet high, four hundred thousand square feet."

"Oh, my God," I gasped.

"I tell you, Celess, I never seen anything like it."

"Who has?"

"They say it'll be the costliest house in the world. They're estimating it at close to two billion."

"Wow," I said, sincerely impressed, but at the same time I was thinking about how the hell Si-Si and I could meet this Mukesh guy. He was a man we needed to know.

"The first six floors are parking garages. Then there are nine elevators in the lobby. They got a big ballroom in there, lounges, an entertainment level, a health spa, panoramic views of the Arabian Sea, gardens, everything." Michael was mesmerized.

He always did love his job, I thought.

"Sounds like big shit you're doing," I told him.

He chuckled. "Yeah, well, enough about me. What are you doing now? Are you in the clear or what? What's your situation?"

"I'm running a business and just staying off the radar, you know." I was vague. "But I'm out here for fashion week."

"When is that? I mean, like how long are you going to be out here? I would love to take you out, show you some of the city that I discovered since being here," he said.

"A few days," I told him. "I'm sure we can make that happen."

"Yes, please, let's. But, uh, I know you're probably tired, having just gotten in and all. I don't want to hold you. What's your room number, though? I'll call you later, and maybe we can meet back up."

I started to give him the number but then thought against it. "How about you give me yours?"

He did, and I repeated it back to him. Then after another tight hug, we started to part ways.

"I'll see you later, Celess," he reiterated.

"Do me a favor," I said. "Call me Bella."

"Bella? Doesn't that mean beautiful, or something like that?"

I smiled and said, "Yeah."

"Well, in that case, I have no problem calling you Bella," he charmed.

I blushed at his corny but genuine way of complimenting me, and I had flashbacks of how special he always made me feel. I was so tingly inside that for the remainder of the day I could hardly sleep. Knowing that Michael was in the same hotel as me had me anxious. I wanted to spend more time with him, talk to him more, and feel that sense of security and love he always provided. I longed for him.

And for the rest of our trip in Mumbai my focus had switched. Yeah, I went to Fashion Week and did some networking, but during each show I was ready for it to be over so that I could meet up with Michael afterward and hang out with him.

While we were at one of the shows, Si-Si met a guy. He was a young Arab guy who looked good as shit. He had dark curly hair and a dark scruffy mustache and beard. He was average height for a guy, about five nine. He had a small but defined build. It was clear he worked out and lifted weights. He wore tailored suits at the shows, but at night when we would see him at the after parties he would be in crushed linen. One night Si-Si approached him about his predictable wardrobe, and I guessed they hit it off. Two nights in a row she had spent time with him after the shows while I was off with Michael. We would meet each other back at our hotel suite in the wee hours of the morning and have girl talk about what we'd done and where we'd gone. Then we would fall asleep to awake and do it all over again.

We were enjoying ourselves. It was a chance for us both to get our minds off our recent loss. And it helped put Si-Si and me back in good graces. I could tell that there was a strain lifted off our friendship—a strain that hadn't even been lifted after our heart-to-heart at the airport in Cape Town.

It was the last day of Fashion Week, October 24, and it just so happened it was Michael's thirty-fifth birthday. His roommate, who was also one of his colleagues, left an invitation for me with the concierge. It was a surprise gathering at Zenzi, a contemporary Asian-inspired restaurant/lounge in a suburb called Bandra, known as the haven of the rich and famous.

I invited Si-Si and her newfound friend, Amir, who agreed to go as long as his bodyguard could accompany us. The four of us rode together to the dinner party, and it was then that I got to see just how much Si-Si and Amir liked each other. They kissed and fondled the whole ride there, as if they were alone in the backseat. It was like watching two teenage lovebirds. Not even Michael and I showed so much public affection toward each other, and we'd known each other longer. I couldn't blame Si-Si, though. Amir was very attractive and was an heir to an oil tycoon in Dubai, so I assumed he was very rich. He reminded me of a younger, darker Andrew, but with older, greener money. Si-Si sure knew how to pick 'em. Lucky bitch. And I meant that in the most endearing way possible.

From time to time Amir's bodyguard and I would exchange glances of disgust at Si-Si and Amir's exaggerated passion. It seemed we both couldn't wait to arrive at Zenzi so we would no longer be forced to watch them practically have sex with their clothes on.

We finally got to the nightspot fifteen minutes before Michael was expected to show. According to one of the guys who worked at his firm with him, Michael was under the impression that he was coming to a business meeting called by his boss. I couldn't wait to see the look on his face once he realized he was actually walking into a surprise party for himself. But unfortunately, I would not get the chance.

Just as Si-Si and I were walking into the lounge, Si-Si's phone started ringing. She dug around in her tortoise shell–

toned patent-leather Gucci Hysteria hobo until she landed on her phone. She pulled it out and looked at the screen.

"It's Cliff," she said nonchalantly. "Hello . . . hello." After the third hello she took the phone away from her ear and looked at the screen again.

"Oh, he hung up," she said.

Meanwhile, my phone began ringing. I was able to answer it right away because I was actually holding it in my hand. It couldn't fit in my Christian Louboutin Cancan satin clutch.

"Hello," I answered.

That's Cliff? Si-Si mouthed to me.

I nodded.

"Celess, I booked you and Si-Si on a flight out tonight. Y'all have to get back here immediately," he said, an intense note of urgency in his voice.

"Why, Cliff? What's wrong?"

Si-Si wrinkled her face as she looked at me, anxiously waiting for me to fill her in.

"I don't want to talk to you about it over the phone. Just the two of you be on the eleven-twenty flight to Cape Town International."

"Okay," I said reluctantly. Then I hung up. I was staring into space, trying to think of all the things that could have possibly gone wrong back home to bring about Cliff's phone call.

"What happened?" Si-Si asked.

"I don't know. But Cliff put us on a flight out tonight and said we needed to get back there right away."

"What the hell?" Si-Si asked.

"Whatever it is, he didn't wanna say over the phone."

"Shit," Si-Si said. "What do you think it is?"

I shook my head. "I don't know."

"What's the departure time?" Si-Si asked, looking at her La Dona gold Cartier watch.

"Eleven-twenty."

"Then we gotta leave now. Like *right* now."

"I know."

Without wasting any more time, Si-Si and I left Zenzi, but not before Si-Si apologized to Amir and made sure they each had all of the other's contact information. I was able to leave my cell number and e-mail address along with the birthday card and small gift I had gotten for Michael with one of his colleagues. As bad as I wanted to be there to help him celebrate his birthday, I couldn't. At least I did get the opportunity to get him a meaningful gift, despite Si-Si's opinion that, if I was going to spend over $2,000 on a gift for him, it sure as hell *shouldn't* have been a pen. I tried to explain to the girl that it was an ivory-and-rose-gold Vermeil roller-ball pen made by Tibaldi, which, as an architect who loved what he did, he could appreciate. I just wished I could be there to see him open it.

Instead, I had to rush back to Cape Town to a situation I never saw coming. None of us had seen it coming.

"Sammy was murdered." The words leaped off Cliff's tongue the minute he saw us in the baggage claim area of Cape Town International Airport.

My mind literally went blank after hearing those words, which were starting to sound too familiar to me. I just dropped my head in the palm of my hands. As for Si-Si, she was frozen. She showed no reaction whatsoever. Just paralyzed. And poor Cliff, who had also recently lost somebody else dear to him, looked like he had been crying for days. His eyes were red and weary, and the skin around them was swollen.

I had a million questions as to how, what, where, when, and why. I just couldn't seem to get them out at that time. It was hard enough wrapping my head around the fact that Sammy had been killed. That was mind-boggling to me. But then again, it was becoming my norm. And as I stood there in that airport, I thought to myself, Who's next?

November 2008

It had been a week since Cliff received a call from a homicide detective at the Orlando Police Department telling him that his number was one of the last ones in Sammy's call log and that he had been killed, but we were just now getting the details of his death. Up until that point Si-Si swore it was her fault. She started to believe that because everyone close to her was dying, maybe she was cursed or something. She started telling everybody to stay away from her, to go about their lives without her in it—scaring the shit out of Lisha and Naja. But I had to explain to her and everybody else that it was pure coincidence. And that based on Sammy's stealing money from his client and other things he may have been into, there was no telling who wanted him dead. Si-Si couldn't put his murder on herself. She couldn't take that charge. I wasn't going to let her. So I decided to track down the client Sammy went to see in Orlando and try to get some information out of her.

After going through some of Sammy's belongings, I came across a number for a Fantasy Cut Kids Salon and Spa in Orlando. I figured it had be the business of his client. I dialed the number and put it on speakerphone for us all to hear.

"Good morning, Fantasy Cut. Would you like to make an appointment?" a woman's voice greeted us.

"Hi," I began, trying to think of the girl's name I had heard Sammy mention. "Um, is um, the owner available?" I finally asked.

"Who's calling?" the lady asked.

"My name is Bella."

"Bella, do you mind my asking the nature of this call?"

"Um . . . It's personal," I said, not wanting to come out asking a perfect stranger about a murder.

Then Si-Si blurted out, "It's regarding Sammy."

"Oh," the lady gulped. "Please hold."

A few seconds went by, and another female voice was heard through the speakerphone.

"Hello, this is Leah, how can I help you?"

That's right, Leah, I thought to myself. "Hi, Leah. My name is Bella. I was a close friend of Sammy's."

"Oh really? Well, I'm sorry about your loss," she said.

"Thank you. I was actually calling to see if you had any information about his murder. I mean, the police are being very vague with us. And we are a ways away from Florida, so it's not like we can come there and investigate ourselves, you know. We just wanna know what happened to him. He was very close to us," I explained.

"Well, I'm sure you know he came here to meet with me to help me with the accounting for my business . . ."

"Um-hum."

"One night we all went out to dinner, and before we left each other, we made plans to meet the next day at the bank to open my business accounts. When he was no call no show, my fiancé and I went to the hotel where he was staying, and that's when we seen that it was a crime scene."

"So he was killed at his hotel?" I wanted to clarify.

"According to the police, he was in the parking lot of his hotel. He was sitting in the car he rented. And an unknown gunman approached the driver's side and shot him in the side of his head point-blank . . ."

Si-Si cringed. Cliff gasped. Tears gathered in Lisha's eyes as she shook her head, and Naja just had a blank stare. Me, I listened intently to every detail, trying to make sense of the crime that took Sammy from us.

"His wallet was on the floor, and it was emptied. And his briefcase was on the backseat. It was emptied as well. They think it was a robbery turned homicide," she explained.

"Oh, my God." I sighed. "Did they say anything about suspects?" I didn't want to leave any stone unturned.

"No. Not to me anyway. They were dusting the scene for fingerprints. Hopefully, whoever did it was dumb enough to leave some."

"Well, thank you so much for taking time out and giving me this information. At least now I can have a little closure."

"No problem," Leah said.

"Good-bye," I started to hang up.

"Oh, wait a minute," Leah came back. "The cops took his cell phone, and they noticed a number in his log that called him back to back the night before and the day of his killing. They tracked the number, and asked me if I knew the guy whose number it was and I said no . . ."

Si-Si's face frowned up as she mouthed to me, *Ask her what his name was.*

"What was the guy's name?" I asked Leah.

"Hold on. Let me get the paper," she said.

In that moment my heart was beating fast. I felt uneasy all of a sudden.

"Hello?" Leah came back to the phone.

"Yeah, I'm here."

"His name was Chatman—"

At that my hand automatically released my cell phone. It dropped to the kitchen floor with so much force the screen cracked. Si-Si's body crumbled and holding her stomach, she started throwing up.

"Hello . . . hello?" Leah's voice could be heard through the speakerphone. Then a click.

While Lisha helped Si-Si to her feet and Naja started to clean up the vomit, Cliff turned to me.

"Who was that guy? Somebody you two know? What is it that caused both of you to react in this way? Is there something we should know, Celess?"

I couldn't answer any of Cliff's questions, partly because I didn't know how to answer them without letting him know Si-Si's and my secret, and partly because I was still trying to grasp the fact that maybe Si-Si was right. Maybe she was the reason behind people close to her dying. She may not have been cursed, but she was a target, and anybody who was in close proximity to her was bound to be hit.

Soon after Si-Si had up her guts, she jumped up from the dining chair and started mapping things out. It was as if somebody had pushed her panic button.

"All right, listen," she freaked. "Cliff, I'm goin' need you to book me a flight out of here, like right now."

"What? Where to?"

"I don't fuckin' know!" Si-Si threw her hands up. "Somewhere!"

"Si-Si, take a breath." I stepped in. "Don't make no sudden moves."

"Celess, you don't know this man like I do. If I don't make a sudden move, then it'll be my ass in a grave," she said to me straight up. "For all I know, he's outside that door waiting for me."

"Who is this guy?" Cliff asked, frustration in his tone.

"He's the man responsible for having my father killed, my mother killed, for trying to have me killed, and now Sammy . . ." Si-Si confessed. "And hell, it may have even been him who had Ryan killed," she hypothesized. Then she hurled over again and threw up. "I gotta get outta here." She wiped her mouth with the back of her hand.

"Oh, my God. This is crazy," Cliff said.

"What should we do?" Lisha asked, concerned.

"If I was any of y'all, I would fuckin' leave. If it was Chatman who had anything to do with Sammy, trust me he's on his way here—"

"He might not be, though," I was trying to sort through my thoughts and help Si-Si make rational decisions. "I mean, how would he know where to come. He caught up with Sammy all the way in Orlando. He could think you're out there too."

"That girl said that his wallet and briefcase were emptied. I'm sure Sammy had at least one piece of paper with this address on it. And even if he didn't, I know Sammy. Any sign of danger weakens him. Chatman's presence alone could have gotten him to rat me out, let alone having a gun to his head," Si-Si theorized. Then she instantly turned to Cliff. "Cliff, book me a flight now!" she demanded.

"Where are you gonna go?"

"What about the business?" Lisha asked.

"You can have the fuckin' business," Si-Si said. She was like a tyrant, pacing about.

"Where do you wanna go?" Cliff asked, punching keys on the laptop.

"Wait, let's think this through," I tried my luck at getting Si-Si to strategize one more time. "We need to take all the money out the accounts. Shut the business down for a minute. Relocate somewhere. And once things simmer, we can rebuild." I went over the steps that we had taken once before.

"The story of our lives," Si-Si said. "All he's going to do is track us down again."

"So what do you suggest?" I asked.

"I suggest we all go our separate ways and pretend we never knew each other," she said with a serious look on her face.

Was she crazy? I thought. Like I was just going to go wandering around in the big world all alone without money, without a plan, without a place to rest my head.

"I don't think so, Si-Si."

"You have no choice, Celess. Now we'll divvy the money and each go our own way. Cliff, check the accounts."

Cliff said okay and started punching the keys on the laptop again.

Lisha was sitting on the couch biting her nails. Naja was mopping and humming under her breath, as if she was trying to force herself to focus on something other than the drama at hand.

"Huuuuhhhhh . . ." Cliff gasped. He looked like he had seen a ghost.

I got up from the bar stool I was sitting on and rushed over to the dining table where he was sitting, kicking my phone by accident along the way. I stood over his shoulder. "What the fuck?"

"How much is missing?" Si-Si asked softly, as if she was afraid to hear the answer.

"All of it," Cliff choked.

"How did that motherfucker get access?" I was outraged. Now my panic button had been pushed. This nigga had fucked with my money, which, as far as I was concerned, was life threatening. Unlike most people, money was everything to me. It was the one thing that helped me survive whenever all odds were against me. It became life support for me, and without it I might as well die.

Si-Si's legs trembled as she sat in a dining chair. "He's trying to trap us here," she said.

"How did he get the money?" Lisha rephrased my question.

"Sammy," Si-Si said. "The police are right. It was a robbery turned homicide."

"But it wasn't like Sammy had one point six in his pocket," Cliff said, sniffling.

"He had him wire it somewhere, I bet you," Si-Si said. "Then they drove back to the hotel, and Sammy probably thought he was off the hook. But he should've known Chatman wasn't going to leave him alive. He should've known."

"So now what?" Cliff asked.

"We wait," Si-Si said.

"Wait for what?" Cliff asked.

"Wait for him. He's coming, and when he does, it'll be what it'll be," Si-Si sounded like she was ready to give up. And whenever she got in one of those moods, I had to be the one to break her out of it.

"Nah, fuck that!" I said. I stood up. "I got a couple dollars that we can use to get us out of here."

They all looked to me like I was a savior.

I ran up to my bedroom and grabbed my Louis bag from one of the shelves in my walk-in closet. I opened it up and took the envelope with the nine checks out of it. I ran back downstairs.

"I had these put aside for a rainy day," I said, holding the checks up.

"It's four thirty. Banks are closed," Si-Si said, unenthused. "Which account are they from anyway?"

"The one we had with Andrew," I answered. "What about check-cashing places?"

"They don't have them here," Lisha chimed in.

"Wasn't there a check card for that account?" Si-Si remembered.

"Fuck, yeah," I said, turning around and running back up the steps. Instead of just getting the check card from the bag, I took the whole bag downstairs with me, because I'd be damned if I was running back up the steps for anything else.

"We can book flights with this," Cliff exclaimed as I held up the check card.

"Is there still money on it?" Si-Si asked. "Those funds are probably depleted by now," she said pessimistically.

I walked over, picked my cracked phone up off the floor, and was lucky to be able to call the number on the back of the card. I followed the prompts and waited anxiously to hear the account balance.

"Your available balance is one hundred fifty-eight thousand, four hundred fifty euros," the automated voice said, music to my ears.

"There's not only money in the account," I told the group.

"There's more than double what was in there since the last time I checked it."

"What?" Si-Si quizzed. "That can't be right."

"Are we goin' to use it to book flights or what before that too suddenly disappears?" Cliff spoke up.

"I am," I said.

"Me too," Lisha said.

"I guess I have to," Naja replied.

"All right, one at a time. Who's first and where to?" Cliff asked.

We all remained silent, assuming that Si-Si would be the first to book.

"Si-Si, you go 'head."

"I'm not booking a flight," she said.

"Why not? You're the one who wanted to in the first place."

"It's a trap."

"What's a trap?"

"Andrew is feedin' that account. He's baitin' us," she said. "Y'all can do it. But I'm not." She was somber.

That was Si-Si being Si-Si whenever the world seemed to be falling on her shoulders. I figured I would talk some got damn sense into her, but later, after everybody booked their flights.

"Well, somebody go then," I said.

"I'll go first," Cliff said. "I'd rather take my chances with Andrew than that Chatman guy."

"Where are you going?" Lisha asked Cliff.

"Back to Italy," he said, punching keys.

"What about you?" he asked her.

She shrugged her shoulders. "Not sure yet."

"What about you, Naja?"

"I guess I'll go back to Brooklyn," she said, tears in her eyes.

"What's out there?" Lisha asked.

"It's my home. It's where I know the streets."

"Okay, Celess, give me the card," Cliff said, his hand out.

I put the card in his palm.

He typed the numbers off the card, pressed a few more buttons, and then looked at me.

"I'm on a red eye," he said. "Brooklyn for you, right, Naja?"

"Yeah, Brooklyn, New York."

"There's an eight thirty-four flight." He looked at Naja.

She nodded. "I'll take it."

"Okay. Spell your name first and last as it appears on your ID," Cliff said.

"Rebecca Simms. R-E-B-E-C-C-A. Simms, S-I-M-M-S," Naja gave him her false identity.

Cliff proceeded booking her flight. Then he turned to Lisha. "Are you ready?"

"I don't need a flight," she said. "I'll take a metro to the city and then hop a rikki back to my family's house."

"You sure," Cliff asked.

"Yeah, I'm sure," she said. "It's where I know the streets, you know," she said, taking a page from Naja's book.

"All right, well, Celess, that leaves you." Cliff looked up at me.

"Hold off on me," I said, glancing over at Si-Si, who was sitting at the table with her head down. "Let's figure out what we'll each get when we split this money."

"We just have to divide it by four," Cliff said.

"No shit, Cliff," I was in no mood for dumb-ass-ness. "Calculate it and tell me what you get," I instructed as I turned to a blank check in my checkbook, which I had retrieved from the bag I'd brought downstairs.

"Okay, uh," Cliff muffled as he punched keys on the laptop.

"One hundred fifty what?"

"One fifty-eight, four fifty," I told him.

"Okay, divided by four, comes to thirty-nine thousand, six hundred twelve, and fifty cents."

"Okay, I'm gonna write each of us a check in that amount," I said, making the first one out to myself.

"Give mine to Naja," Si-Si said, her head still down on the table.

"What?" Naja asked, surprised.

"You need it more than me. Just do right by it."

"Oh, my God, Si-Si, thank you so much!" Naja cried. "Thank both of y'all so much."

"Wow," Lisha said. "I was fuckin' the wrong one," she smirked.

I shot her a shut-the-fuck-up look. She understood and tried to recover by changing the subject.

"So what are you gonna do with your money, Naja?"

Naja walked over to me to get her check, and after looking at it she shared her plans. "I'm gonna go get my little brother and my sister's son from foster care, and I'm gonna raise them up in a nice house like my sister always wanted," she said, tears escaping her eyes.

"Awww, that's nice," Lisha said. "In that case, I'm glad Si-Si chose you to give her share to. You deserve it, you hear me? You are such a young girl, and already you've been through so much. I wish you nothing but peace and happiness from here. I pray your struggles are behind you."

Naja, consumed with emotion, fell into Lisha's arms. She cried while Lisha patted her back. And right then I had a moment of clarity. Naja was only fourteen or fifteen years old—just a child—and she had seen and been through more things than an average person does in a lifetime. Despair had been hand delivered to that poor girl at a very young age. And me, a person who had a pretty normal upbringing, I seemed to welcome despair with open arms, and in some cases I even created it. I wondered how healthy that was, or if it was healthy at all. And I figured it couldn't be. After all, my choices and selfish decisions had almost cost me my life on numerous occasions. I figured, No more. I was truly ready to make a change. I couldn't keep taking my life for granted, especially knowing that there were so many people out there who would give their lives to have mine.

"Here you go, Lisha. Here you go, Cliff," I handed the two of them their checks.

"So what are you and Si-Si going to do?" Cliff asked. "Do y'all want me to book y'all a flight somewhere?"

"I'll take care of it," I told him.

"Are you sure?" he asked. "Where are y'all going to go?"

"I'll take care of it," I reiterated. "I think y'all should just go start packing. Naja's going to need one of y'all to take her to the airport."

At my suggestion, Cliff, Lisha, and Naja all dispersed to their bedrooms.

Meanwhile, Si-Si was still at the table with her head buried in her arms.

"Si-Si." I got her attention.

"Hum?"

"I know that you feel like you have no win. But how many times have you felt this exact way before but managed to come out victorious?" I tried dealing with her on a mental level first, before getting physical and forcing her out of the house and onto a plane. That would be my last resort.

Si-Si lifted her head. "I hear you, Celess. I just don't have no more fight in me. Especially against him. Now if this was anybody else, I would probably stand tall, but not against Chatman. That man been making my life hell since I was five years old, Celess." Her eyes were sincere.

I sat down in the chair next to Si-Si. I reached my hands out and placed them on her knees.

"What was it that you said to me when O had worn me down to the point where I felt like giving up? Huh? You told me to fight fire with fire," I reminded her. "And since I've met you, that was what you've been known for. Chatman may be relentless, but he's only one man. We're two bad ass bitches—"

Si-Si smirked.

"Seriously," I said, trying to regain her focus. "We've taken down mutherfuckas before. And there's no reason why we can't do it again." I paused to let her think about what I was saying and hopefully gain confidence in it. "Now, all we gotta do is leave here and go somewhere quiet, where we can think this thing through, and then when the snake rears his ugly head, we'll be ready to strike."

She twisted her lips and obviously gave thought to what I was saying.

"For your sake, Celess, I will. I will follow your lead. But please, I beg you to forgive me now if, in fact, you turn out to be wrong," she said.

Si-Si's words shook me to the core. They spelled out the fact that there was actually a chance that I would be killed just for being associated with her. For a split second I wondered if it were worth it. If riding out with her would be worth my losing my life. I didn't think so. And something in me told me to get up, walk out the door, and leave Si-Si where she sat. But when I asked myself whether Si-Si would ride out with me and the answer I came to was yes, I realized I had to do the same. My heart wouldn't allow me to do her dirty a second time.

I took a deep breath then I told her, "You're forgiven."

We then went straight into plan mode.

"So where should we go?" Si-Si asked.

"With just forty grand, we only have two options," I told her. "We can go back to Mumbai and stay with Michael until he finishes his project, or we can call ya homey Amir and go to Dubai."

"Flip a coin," she said without hesitation.

I pulled a quarter from my bag. "Heads, Mumbai. Tails, Dubai."

I tossed the quarter in the air and let it fall on the back of my hand. It landed on tails. Si-Si grabbed her phone off the table and searched her contacts list until she got to Amir's number. She made the international call, and we prayed he'd pick up.

After a few rings, he did. And based on Si-Si's facial expression, he was cool with our coming to see him. He gave Si-Si an address, and she hung up.

I opened up the laptop, restarted it, and booked us a one-

'Til Death

way flight to Dubai International. We packed our most important belongings. Then we said our good-byes to Cliff, Lisha,
and Naja. Hugs, tears, and well wishes were exchanged. Then
Si-Si and I left the million-dollar home we had lived in in a
suburb of Cape Town, South Africa. Our journey, I thought to
myself as we got in the minibus that we had called to take us to
the airport. Our mutherfuckin' journey.

Dubai was like a paradise. The sun seemed to shine forever, and the seas were always gleaming. But aside from the natural beauty it possessed, the man-made wonders that it housed were beautiful and magnificent beyond words. The buildings were constructed with curves and bends and twists that made them look more like art than structures. Then there were the man-made islands—the Palm Islands—which could be seen from space, and the more recently constructed World Islands, three hundred individual islands shaped and placed to look like the world map from an aerial view. To get to these islands you had to travel by boat, seaplane, or helicopter. It was nothing short of amazing.

Si-Si and I took a few weeks just to soak it all in before we discussed one thing about our current situation. I don't think we expected the country to be so hypnotizing. It grabbed hold of us instantly, and it was hard for either one of us to snap out of the sleeplike state it had put us in.

But when we did, it was just in time for more bullshit. Since landing in Dubai, we had been staying in a villa that Amir's family owned on Palm Island. He had put us up nicely. We wanted to stay there forever, but the reality was we posed a threat to Amir. We didn't know if Chatman had an idea of where we were or not, and we didn't want to jeopardize Amir. So we thanked him for his extreme hospitality and moved out of the villa. We booked a modest suite at the Jumeira Emirates Tower at Jumeira Beach. It was the first time in a long time we stayed somewhere that cost only $230 per night.

We checked into the hotel, which was to be our residence for at least the next thirty days, and despite its low price tag, it was very luxurious and modern. We had no complaints.

As soon as we got in the suite, we ordered room service. We were starving. Si-Si jumped in the shower, and I started unpacking my clothes. Halfway through putting my clothes in the drawers and closets, I heard a knock at the door.

I stopped what I was doing and went to answer it. I didn't peep through the peephole because I assumed it was our food.

I opened the door and was shocked to see Andrew standing in front of me. My instinct told me to hurry and shut the door. But when I tried, he intercepted, pushing it open with all his strength. He forced himself in the suite, putting the top lock on the door as it closed.

I was scared to death. I didn't know what he was doing there, how he had found us, and if Chatman was close behind.

He didn't say anything right away. He just stared at me with unreadable eyes. Then Si-Si, wrapped in a plush robe, walked into the living space where we were having a stare down. Upon seeing Andrew, her cheerful pace came to a sudden halt.

"Andrew?" she blurted fearfully.

Andrew shook his head. "You two," he finally broke his silence. "What on God's earth are you two doing? Do you have any idea what you've gotten yourselves into? I mean, you come out to Rome and stay with me in my home and not tell me that you were running from the police for a murder? Then you go into business with me. You put my life, my business, my whole existence in jeopardy, then you steal my car, flee, and then drain one of my bank accounts." He laid it all out.

"Look, Andrew," Si-Si jumped in, "for what it's worth, we're truly sorry, and as for the money, you can have it back. I knew we shouldn't have taken it in the first place. I knew it was bait." Si-Si obviously figured the money was how Andrew tracked us down.

"It's not about the money, Sienna. You know that little bit of money means nothing to me. Besides, you're right, it was bait. I deposited five thousand euros into the account every week since you two disappeared on me. I knew it was just a matter of time until you would need it or just want it. I just waited patiently for that time to come. And finally I got alerted that there was some activity and that several flights had been booked using the account—Florence, Brooklyn, and Dubai. I knew you two were not dumb enough to go back to the States, where your faces are probably plastered everywhere. And Florence was out of the question too. I mean, you two would have to be fools to come anywhere near Rome. So Dubai it was. I came here three and a half weeks ago but," he said with a smirk, "I couldn't locate you because you didn't use the card or any checks the whole time—until today. You finally booked a hotel."

"Andrew, we're so sorry," Si-Si said. "We never intended for you to be in the middle of our nonsense."

Then Si-Si broke out in Italian, apparently pleading with Andrew to forgive us and have mercy on us.

"*Mi dispiace*," she whined. "*Non homai voluto portare alcun danno! Sapete che! Vi prego di credermi!*"

I was lost in translation, but I could tell that whatever Si-Si was spitting to Andrew it was working on him. He had a pitiful look on his face.

"Sienna, Sienna, Sienna," he said. "You are a one of a kind. Stop whining. I know you meant me no harm. And that's why I'm even here. Because something inside me knows that you are truly a good person who was just dealt a raw deal. I wanna help you like always, but you didn't let me when you kept something so big and crucial from me like that."

"And I realize that, Andrew. I do. I wish I had been up front with you when I came out to your house. That would've been the fair thing to do, even if you would've turned your back on me. I should've given you the right to choose."

"*Esattamente.* Exactly," Andrew said. "Now here's your chance to redeem yourself. I want you to tell me what I need to know. I mean, after Ron told me that you two were supposedly on the run after killing a guy, I looked online and read up on the case. I didn't believe him, not even after Celess took off with my car. I was still in disbelief. What happened back there in Los Angeles?"

"Sit down, Andrew," Si-Si said.

Andrew reluctantly took a seat on the desk chair that sat opposite the couch. Si-Si sat on the couch and I sat on its arm.

"Celess and I were shot at during my grandmother's burial in L.A. We thought it was retaliation from one of Celess's exes. We made arrangements to leave the country for a short while, just until things cooled down. And that was when I called you and asked if we could visit. Then the day that we were scheduled to leave, we went to my house to get my mom, and she was in the—" Si-Si began to choke up.

I rubbed her back to offer what little comfort I could.

"My mom was lying in a pool of blood. She was dead. And Celess and I had to get out of there because we just knew that whoever did it was still there and was waiting to kill us. So we were on our way to the car when a guy came out of nowhere and pointed a gun at Celess's head. I didn't know what else to do but take the gun that I kept in my house and shoot him in his back." Si-Si told the story as best she could remember. Then she broke into tears. "I never meant to kill anybody. I never wanted to do that. I was just scared, and he was going to kill Celess. And he had just killed my mom. And since that day my life has been a nightmare. I mean, yeah, I was able to live good and travel, and shop, and have fun, but at the end of the day, the fact that I am on the run from the police for a murder eats away at me," Si-Si revealed.

"Well, Sienna, honey, I'm sorry to tell you," Andrew said, moving onto the couch. He sat beside Si-Si and, as bluntly as possible, told her, "*La polizia* are the least of your worries."

Si-Si wiped her face and looked up at Andrew. "I know that," she said. "But how do *you* know that?"

"After I found out what you two had done, I set a Google alert with your names so that any press mentioning you would come to me in my e-mail. Well, like a week or so after the whole incident at the movie set, I got a bunch of e-mails with press about you two. Most were stories about the murder over a year ago and the fact that you all were never found. But one story stood out from the rest, and it's why I'd been determined to track you down. It said that a woman was found brutally murdered in her Philadelphia home—"

At that my mind began racing. I kept mumbling beneath my breath: Not my mom, please, God, not my mom.

"Apparently this woman was a psychologist, and one of her clients, a guy named—"

Okay, wait a minute, I thought, my mom isn't a psychologist. My mom was never a psychologist.

"Carlos Vasquez went to the authorities because he believed his estranged brother, who had been in trouble with the law since they were kids, may have had something to do with this woman's death. He explained to the cops that, a day after this woman was seen live on a *World News* broadcast pleading for you, Celess, to call her or to come home and turn yourself in, his brother had called him and was like, wasn't that lady on TV your shrink? And apparently he told the brother yeah, you know, why? And the brother was just like, I want to seek treatment from her when I get out of jail. Can you give me her information? And so the guy gave his brother this lady's telephone number, you know, thinking he was just trying to better himself. Then about a day or two after that the guy, Carlos Vasquez, said he got a call from his psychologist. She asked him how his brother knew of her client Celess—"

"Wait a minute," I interrupted. "So it's saying that the woman was my psychologist?"

Andrew nodded slowly. "That's what I got from it."

"Not Ms. Carol." I didn't want to accept that, and I wasn't

going to. That was bullshit. This was all just a fuckin' prolonged nightmare that would have to end soon, I told myself.

"Carol was her name," Andrew stated, as he stood up to pull some papers from his jeans pocket. It was a news article.

I read the headline aloud, "Four years after Carlos Vasquez's alleged mistress commits suicide, his family's psychologist is murdered."

"Oh, my God! Who would do that to Ms. Carol?" I broke down. "She never did anything to anybody!"

"I'm confused," Si-Si said. "Who is this Carlos? And what does he have to do with you knowing that the police are the least of my worries?"

"Well, the brother Carlos believes killed his psychologist was named Chatman."

"So Chatman killed Ms. Carol?" Si-Si didn't seem to comprehend. "But why?"

"According to the article, Carlos got a call from the psychologist. She told him that his brother had come to see her and asked about a client of his by the name of Celess. She told him she didn't know where Celess was, and the next day she was dead. So this Carlos guy doesn't know why Chatman was looking for Celess, but he speculates that that was the real reason he wanted the psychologist's information to begin with. But we know why Chatman would be interested in finding Celess."

"To get to me," Si-Si got it.

"*Esattamente*," Andrew said. "That's why I came out here. It wasn't about the money. It wasn't even about you keeping me in the dark. I had to try to get to you two before he did. To let you know what you were up against."

I was too busy sobbing to thank Andrew for being con

cerned enough to risk his life to help us. I couldn't bear the thought of Ms. Carol suffering a brutal death behind my saga. I was tormented by it. I had never experienced such internal pain; not even when Tina died did I feel as horrible as I did at that moment. I mean, damn. This nigga was ruthless, I thought of Chatman. He was stopping at nothing. And the more I thought about just how evil he had to be to do what he did to an innocent woman like Ms. Carol, the more desperate I became to see this nigga's brains be blown out. I was livid. I felt like I could explode.

"You two need to turn yourselves in to the police. At least then you will be safe from Chatman. Then once you get in custody, let the police focus on getting Chatman back behind bars where he belongs," Andrew suggested.

"Celess, I'm so sorry," Si-Si cried as she tried to cradle my weeping self in her arms. "This is all my fault. Like I said before, all these innocent people are being killed because of me. No more," she said. She kissed me on my forehead. Then she turned to Andrew and kissed him on his cheek.

She stood up from the couch.

"Where are you going?"

"I'm gonna take your advice," she said.

"You're gonna go to the police?"

She nodded, tears pouring down her face.

"You want me to take you?"

"No," she shook her head. "I want you to leave. Go back to Rome. Cut all ties to me. I can't have anybody else's blood on my hands."

Andrew took a hard swallow. He stood up and pulled Si-Si into him. He squeezed her as hard as he could without hurting her.

"When you get to where you're going, write me. I will take care of you, you hear me? I will always take care of you," he whispered.

Andrew then leaned down and hugged me. "Celess, you too need to go to the police. This man is very dangerous. I'd rather get a Google alert that you two have turned yourselves in than one saying you two have been killed. *Please*. For your own sakes."

I didn't say anything. I just cried.

Andrew stood back up. "I love you guys," he said, a crack in his voice. Then he took the top lock off the door and walked out of the hotel suite.

Si-Si left the living room and went into the bedroom. I could hear her moving around. She must have been getting dressed.

I wanted to get off the couch, but I couldn't. I was too emotional. Even when there was a knock at the door and a voice calling, "Room service," I didn't budge. I just sat there drowning in tears and guilt.

Si-Si had emerged from the bedroom fully dressed. She too ignored the knocking, and eventually it stopped. She had a duffel bag in one hand and her cell phone in the other.

"Celess, what are you going to do?" she asked me. Her face was pale, and her eyes were bloodshot. "You can't stay here. It's only a matter of time before he sniffs us out."

"I'm gonna leave," I cried. "I just need a second."

"Are you goin' to the police?" she asked.

I was hesitant answering that. Then I asked, "Are you?"

She nodded.

"Well, I guess I am too, then. We might as well go together."

"We can't, Celess," Si-Si said.

"Why not?" I looked up at her, confused.

"Because, don't you get it? The longer you're around me, the more likely it is for Chatman to get to you." She paused, her eyes roaming the room. Then she added, "And not only do I not want to see anything happen to you on account of me, but I know how much you value your life, Celess. Let's split up so you can have a better chance."

I thought about what Si-Si was saying, and while she seemed to be taking my life into consideration, she also seemed to be taking a shot at me on the slide.

"Is this your way of paying me back for when I left you at the airport in Rome? Huh? Is that why you really wanna split up? I mean, 'cause if you were just going to the police like you say, it wouldn't be a big deal for us to go together. And besides, who takes a duffel bag of clothes to jail? You're not going to the police. You just want me to," I figured.

"You're right, Celess. I'm not goin' to turn myself in. But I do want you to. And not because of what you did to me in Rome. This has nothing to do with that. I'm past that. This is about me caring a hell of a lot about you and not wanting to see you end up dead like all the other people who I've ever cared about in my life. If you stay on the streets, it'll be just a matter of time before your luck will run out. You know that, and I know that, Celess."

"Okay, so if that's the case, what do you think will happen to you if you stay on the streets? You don't think your luck will run out? You think Chatman can catch up with everybody around you but just not you?"

"No, that's not what I think. But if and when I cross that bridge, I am positively certain I can live with whatever shall happen. But I know that's not the case for you. One thing I learned about you when you left me and went to South Africa by yourself was that you cared about your own life a lot more than you cared about mine. And that's how I feel right now, Celess. I care about your life a lot more than I care about mine."

Si-Si's words hit a nerve. She was dead-on. I couldn't argue with her. And no, she was not taking a shot at me, she was just keepin' it one hundred. She was a real girl, probably the realest girl I had ever met. And I could do nothing but respect her and her decision. So while I didn't want to split up that time, I wasn't going to make a fuss out of it. I had to let Si-Si go on without me, just like she had let me go on without her in the past.

"I love you, Si-Si," I told her, standing up to hug her.

"I love you too, Celess," she said, taking a long, hard sniff, as if she was using all her might to fight back tears. "You be safe."

"You be safe too."

"I will. We'll see each other again," she said. Then she opened the door and vanished.

I cried some more, not thinking about the danger I was in, but regretful for the danger I had brought to others—others who, in my opinion, deserved to live more than I did.

Some hours later, when I finally got control of myself and my flood of tears, I got up from the couch and dragged myself into the bedroom. I planned to wash my face and clean up a little. Then I was going to call the police for them to come and get me.

Seeing Si-Si's clothes scattered all over the bed, some missing, obviously packed into the duffel she took with her, I questioned if I really wanted to turn myself in. I mean, Si-Si was back on the run, and I felt like I needed to be with her. There was no sense in my turning myself in if she wasn't going to. Why would I take the fall by myself? Besides, I had absolutely nothing to lose anymore, so I'd rather take my chances on the streets eluding the cops and Chatman until one of them or both caught up to me.

I packed me an overnight bag as well, grabbed my cell and my charger, and left the hotel. I was going to find Si-Si. We were in this thing together. 'Til death. That was our promise.

I felt myself sobering up as I was wandering the streets of Dubai. It was pitch-black outside, which would have been normal at that hour had it been any other day of the year. But it was New Year's and not one firework sparked the night sky. It was unusual. No outdoor celebrations at all. What the hell? I thought. Was it the end of the world and I didn't get the memo. What country didn't celebrate New Year's?

I noticed a couple go into an Irish pub. I decided to follow them. Maybe there was some spectacle hidden in there. I walked inside. Nope. Nothing. No frills. I walked over to the bar and asked for a shot of vodka. While the bartender poured it, I asked him, "Where are all the New Year's celebrations at? It's twenty minutes pass twelve, and I didn't hear any shots ring out, no fireworks, no parties," I expressed.

"Everything was canceled," the bartender said with a British accent.

"Why?" I questioned, taking the shot he slid over to me.

"To show that we sympathize with the people in Gaza who are suffering right now," he said. "All the big public celebrations and fireworks displays have been canceled. Only private

miasha

parties and hotels are doing things. And it's all indoors this year."

I looked at him like he was speaking a foreign language. "Wow," I said. "So if I were to ask where's the most popular New Year's party, you would say what?" I felt my words slurring and my head pounding. Maybe I wasn't sobering up after all.

"You can try the hotels," he said.

"Which one? Like, where would all the rich and famous people go to celebrate?" I asked him, thinking that of all the places I had searched for Si-Si, including the villa we stayed in together on Palm Island, I was bound to find her at the hottest New Year's event. That was a given. It was what we did, what we looked forward to at year's end. I knew she had to be out celebrating somewhere.

"You can try . . . Le Meridien," he said, seemingly unsure. But what the hell, it was worth a try.

"Thanks," I told him, paying him what I owed for the shot and his tip.

He offered to call me a taxi to take me, and I graciously accepted.

About fifteen minutes and two shots later, the taxi was there to pick me up. I got in the backseat and told the driver where to take me.

I fell asleep on the way to the hotel, extremely exhausted from having gone the last four days without sleep. Just loading up on cocaine, which is the hardest shit to come across in the U.A.E., I had to go to some slum, and even there it was scarce. I found out later that the drug laws were so stiff over there that people were supercautious. I had heard that Dallas Austin was caught with just over a gram and was sentenced to four years in a Dubai prison. Of course, his connects were able to arrange for him to be pardoned, but shit, what if he had been a nobody?

I must admit, I was scared even to think about coke after hearing that story. But my desire to have it overpowered any fear of being caught with it, and I wound up taking the risk.

That was three days after finding out about Ms. Carol. Since then, I had been snorting every day, multiple times a day. I needed to keep my mind from wandering, and the cocaine did just that. It helped me stay clear and focused. In the meantime, I was trying to find Si-Si's ass. Neither she nor Amir had surfaced in the past few weeks. And being as though Amir was such a common name out there, nobody could point me in his direction without a last name. Trying to find him out there was like looking for a Jose in Puerto Rico, but worse. Shit, they even called the prince Amir out in Dubai.

"Le Meridien," the taxi driver said with a loud and heavy accent.

I lifted my head off the window it had been rested on. I sat up, rubbed my face with my palm, which was trembling. I dug in my jeans pocket and pulled out twenty dirham. I had gotten Dubai currency from a drug dealer who agreed to convert my euros for a fee. Don't ask me how much he got me for. I was just trying to hurry up and buy the coke and get the fuck outta there.

"Thank you," I mumbled, getting out of the taxi.

I walked inside Le Meridien, the modern white boxy structure whose name was fluorescently lit. It looked like a nightclub.

There were people mingling and lingering about, almost all of them sipping champagne. I went straight to the concierge. I wanted to find out where the festivities were being held so that I could go look for Si-Si. I didn't have time for anything else.

"Hi, I'm looking for the New Year's party," I said, trying my best to look sober. I heard they locked some lady up just for having drugs in her system, not even in her possession. I wanted no part of it.

"Everything has been pretty much canceled this year." He repeated what the bartender told me at the Irish pub.

"Yeah, I heard about that, but a guy told me to come here for something indoors," I explained, trying to refrain from getting annoyed.

"Well, this is it," he said, motioning toward the ten to fifteen people scattered in the lobby. "Follow these people."

I felt myself growing agitated, so instead of asking the concierge any more questions and risking getting into an argument with his stupid ass, I just walked away from the desk.

I went outside and stood in front of the hotel, catching the breeze. There was a guy out front smoking a cigarette. I glanced over at him a few times. He must have noticed because after like the fifth time he asked, "Are you all right?"

I don't remember what I had replied. I just remember my legs feeling real wobbly like they were going to give out on me. Tears rushed to my eyes, and I broke down crying. I was broken, and I was lost. I was in a totally different world with no one at all. I felt so alone, so scared and destitute. I had been running out of money and bouncing from hotel to hotel, wearing my four outfits over and over. Not getting anything good to eat or getting any sleep. Just been spending my days getting high, drinking, and wandering the streets in search of Si-Si and drugs.

I felt myself being lifted off my feet. The air swept across my face, which felt like it was pressed against the sky. I was shaking and sweating. I felt so irritable.

"Baby girl. Baby girl," the guy who had been smoking outside the hotel was saying as he carried me someplace.

I heard traffic noises, so I knew we were in the street. Then I heard sounds from an alarm keypad when a car door was being unlocked. Next, it was the sound of a door opening, and I felt myself being lowered. The guy, who I got a good look at as he was laying me across the backseat of what I assumed to be his car, was smiling at me. His skinny, long white face and spiked up hair made him look like the '90s rapper Vanilla Ice. And that thought prompted me to ask him if he had any ice.

Thank God he wasn't the police or anybody like that, or my ass woulda been serving time just for asking him something like that, I thought.

"I got everything you could want or need, baby girl," he said as he took his position in the driver's seat.

He started the engine and drove away. What direction we went in, I didn't know. Where he was taking me, I didn't know that either. And at that point in time, I really didn't give a damn.

After what felt like hours, we arrived at a hotel downtown called the Golden Sands. The guy helped me into the hotel, onto the elevator, down the hall, and into his room, which had a bed, a couch, a desk, and a kitchenette. Everything was in one room, basically.

He helped me over to the bed. Then as I was sitting on the edge, rocking back and forth, he offered me a blanket.

"I am cold," I told him.

He untucked the quilt from the top of the bed and tossed it over my shoulders and back. Then he went into the kitchen area and grabbed a bag out of the refrigerator.

He opened the bag and dumped its contents onto the small coffee table that was in front of the couch to my right. Bags of cocaine, weed, and some other substance fell on the table. There were pills, syringes, cotton balls—everything. A little pharmacy had fallen out the bag.

"I just want a couple hits so I can get some sleep," I told him. "I been partying nonstop for days. I don't need no party."

The guy smiled, opening the bag of coke. He took a handful of dollar bills out of his pocket.

"You're American?" I asked him, noticing the money.

"Yeah. Aren't you?" he guessed.

I nodded. I watched him roll one of the dollars tightly until it was a skinny tube. Then he poured the cocaine on the table and lined one end of the dollar up to his nostril and the other end up to the pile of coke. He sniffed. And sniffed. And sniffed until the pile had disintegrated.

"You goin' save some for me?" I asked.

"Of course," he said, getting up from his kneeling position on the floor.

He walked over to me and stood right in front of my face, his midsection touching my nose.

"What are you willing to do for it?" he asked in a whisper.

I smirked. I should've known he was going to try something sexual. I wasn't upset though. He could have easily raped me, but he didn't. So fuck it, I might as well fuck him. I had nothing else planned for that night. And with every big event canceled, I was probably not going to find Si-Si anywhere.

"Just give me a little to scratch this itch, then you can have it your way," I told the American boy.

He handed me the dollar, walked back over to the table, and scooped the remaining cocaine from the table into his palm.

He walked back over to me and held his hand out in front of me. I put the dollar to my nose and to the small pile of drugs. I sniffed twice. Good, good, I thought, feeling better almost instantly.

I lay back and spread my legs apart, giving the guy rights to my body. He proceeded to undress himself and me simultaneously. Before long he was inside me, thrusting his small pelvis back and forth, in and out.

I can't tell you how many times we had sex and how much coke and whatever else we did that morning. All I knew was that I was high as hell. I woke up bright and early on New Year's Day. I had one thing on my mind, to find Si-Si.

I got out the bed, threw my clothes on, and, without waking the guy I had spent the night with, I left the hotel room. I was walking down the hall toward the elevator, and I saw a woman waiting to get on. She was covered from head to toe in Muslim attire. I heard the beep from the elevator indicating it was there, so I called out to her to hold it for me.

She looked at me and removed the veil from her face. And lo and behold it was Si-Si.

"Si-Si!" I shouted with excitement.

Then she said, "The roof," and got on the elevator, allowing it to close without me.

Oh God, I thought. What now? I got to the elevator and pressed the up button.

When it came I got on and pressed the number seven,

which was the highest number on the panel. I waited for it to go up and I got off at my chosen floor. I looked to my left and then my right. And from the corner of my eye I saw the black fabric from Si-Si's garment disappear into a staircase at the end of the hall. I followed it. I went up the two flights of stairs and opened the door at the top.

I walked out onto the roof of the hotel. The downtown skyline was in view. The sun beamed down on all the golden rooftops. I had to squint to be able to see and make my way over to Si-Si, who was standing by the roof's edge.

"Si-Si, I've been looking all over for you! No wonder I couldn't find you. You are all covered up," I joked, feeling a sense of elation after having found her.

"Celess," Si-Si said, looking down on the world below us. "Why do you continue to look for me?" she asked. "Wasn't your plan to turn yourself into the police?"

"Yeah, it was," I said, "But when I realized you weren't going to do it, I didn't want to either. I didn't feel like we should split up again. I felt like we were in this together and so we should've made any decisions together," I told her.

"Well, we're no longer in this together, Celess," Si-Si said, giving me a sudden mood change. "I'm going my way for good, and I want you to go yours, Celess."

Okay, I thought, I had spent all my days looking high and low for this girl so that she wouldn't have to face Chatman or the cops by herself, and she goin' tell me to go my way? Like I'm a flea or a pest or something. Oh, hell no!

"*What about the so-called pact we had? Huh? What happened to that? 'Til death, remember?*" I screamed at Si-Si.

"*This is death!*" she yelled back, then she paused. She looked around to see if our outbursts were bringing any unwanted attention our way. Then she took a second to gather her composure. "Death to Sienna, death to Si-Si, death to Vida," she said in a much lower tone.

"What are you talkin' about, Si-Si?" I asked, too frustrated and too high to figure out any riddles.

"The life we were living is over, Celess. It's a wrap. Give it up. Turn yourself in. The streets are not safe for you."

"And they're safe for you?" I asked. "What, you want me to cover my whole body? Will that make me safe? 'Cause if that's what you want, I'll do it. But I'm not turning myself in!" I said. "Not unless you are!" I added.

"Well, that's your choice," she said, still looking down at the world. "Whatever you decide to do, that's on you."

"Okay, cool. Now that we have that understanding, what are you going to do? I say we hook with some of these rich-ass oil niggas and build us an empire off they dime." I wanted bad to get back the life Si-Si and I had when it was good.

"I'm done with all that, Celess." Si-Si shook her head. "Last night," she began slowly and steadily, as if the words that were about to come off her tongue were fragile. "Amir took me to take my *shadada*. Then this morning we went . . . and got married."

I was in total and utter shock, almost speechless, but I was able to yell out, "*What?!*"

Si-Si looked around again. Then she explained, "Celess, I don't wanna end up like my mom." Tears began to escape her light brown eyes, which was all I could see of her. "Or like all the other women I've known throughout my life. I *want* to grow old someday. I wanna settle down and have children, watch them grow and play and laugh and learn and just witness a normal existence before I leave this earth. And I don't see that happening if I continue on this path. All the sex and the drugs, the alcohol and the partying—it's all a waste," she said, shaking her head. "Wasted energy, wasted money, wasted time. I mean, we had our fun, yes, I'll admit that. But realistically"—she paused, looked down and back up before she continued—"how long will it last?" Si-Si wiped her eyes and took a breath. She shrugged her shoulders and with the most sincere look in her eyes she said, "I want a *real* life, Celess, not just a fast one."

Too bad I wasn't buying it. I mean, not only was it sudden and random, like many decisions Si-Si made, but I was high, and she was blowin' it. I rolled my eyes and folded my arms, resting them across my stomach. I was so ready to dismiss all that Si-Si was saying. I mean, we had been through so much shit together, and for her just to turn her back on me for some nigga she practically just met didn't make any sense to me. I was sure she was just talking out her ass. Amir got in her ear a little bit, broke her off some good dick, and flashed his wealth before her—and she was ready to submit. I was sure she just needed a wake-up call.

"We're still young, Si-Si! You actin' like we 'bout to croak! We have our whole lives to change," I reminded her, thinking about the ten year's minimum that we had left to play with.

Si-Si didn't say anything. She just looked around, her eyes bouncing from one golden dome to the next. I thought I had her and I started to seal the deal with a plan for us both to switch out of the fast lane in 2014. I figured we could agree to at least five more years of making money and moves. But right before I had the chance to propose we make a deal, she said something that sent chills down my spine.

"Celess, you need to get out of the game while you still *have* your life to change."

I unfolded my arms and brought my hands to my face, holding them over my eyes for a second. The last time I heard someone say something like that to me, I didn't take heed. And not only did I come close to death, but I also lost the dearest person to me. In my mind I felt like Si-Si's request of my getting out of the game with her was a sign from God for me to do something different this time, for me to truly stop living the way I was living.

Right then on that rooftop in Dubai, my life with Si-Si up until that moment flashed before my eyes, like scenes from an action movie. There were so many ups and downs, good times and bad, and when I thought about each occurrence, I realized that the downs trumped the ups and the bad times outweighed the good. Not to mention, I was running from two of the most powerful entities under God. How was I to rise from that? Surely not by carrying on the way I had been. Si-Si was right. I needed to make some changes once and for all. And if I were ever to be caught by either of my adversaries, at least I would be able to say I had spent some of my life living right.

"Celess, I have to go," Si-Si said, bringing my deep thoughts to a close.

I thought she was going to turn to me and give me a hug good-bye, but she didn't. Instead, she turned around and walked away from me, her back to me.

"We'll see each other again, right?" I called out to Si-Si.

"*Insha'Allah,*" was her response. "God willing."

I shook my head. I had mixed feelings about everything. I mean, where was I to go from there? Where would Si-Si go from there? Well, at least she was safe, I thought. The rest was up to fate.

I started toward the door to the staircase. I left the rooftop and the hotel altogether. Outside on the street, I noticed a young boy selling newspapers. I decided to buy one and look through it for housing. My money was too low to keep footing hotel bills.

The cover story's headline read, "Future American Starlet Slain While Hiding Out in Dubai." I skimmed through the text and opened to the page where the story continued. I skimmed down that page as well, until I got to the bottom and saw a small picture of Si-Si. Thinking my mind had to be playing tricks on me, I went back to the beginning of the story and started to read. I had just talked to Si-Si. There was no way this paper could be saying she was dead. I even looked at the date of the paper. It was for that day, so there was no way it could be right.

I read it from beginning to end. It said that Si-Si's body had been wrapped in a black sheet and tossed in a Dumpster behind a hotel. It had been discovered weeks ago. Apparently they had ID'd her by her dental records, which had just come back with a positive match to Sienna Alvarez.

As I kept reading, I kept questioning the paper and myself. I was trying to figure out which was a more reliable source. What I had just seen on the roof with my own two eyes or this damn paper?

"Excuse me," I said to the boy who sold me the paper. "Can I have my money back, please? This paper is bogus. It's lies. It's fuckin' sick, demonic lies," I told him, holding my hand out toward him for him to take the paper back.

The boy looked at me like I was crazy. And that was the last thing I remembered before I just blacked out.

*   *   *

I opened my eyes slowly, squinting them, trying to adjust to the bright lights. I heard a constant beeping sound, and above me was an IV bag dangling from a pole. I was in a hospital.

I was lying flat on my back, and I wanted to sit up so that I could see what was going on. I went to push the buttons on the side of the bed that would adjust it to an upright position but realized my hand was cuffed to the bed. I panicked.

"Get me the fuck outta here! What the fuck is this? This some crazy hospital or something? Where the fuck y'all got me at? What the fuck is this?" I went off.

Shortly after I started ranting and raving, a nurse appeared in my room.

"Who the fuck are you, and why the fuck you got me handcuffed to this bed?" I went in on her.

"I'm your nurse. And I'm not the one who cuffed you to the bed. The police did," she explained in a nurturing tone.

"Why? Why did the police cuff me to a bed? And why the hell am I even in the hospital?"

"Your blood tested positive for cocaine," she said, and I remembered the night before. "And high levels, at that," she pointed out.

"Well, what gave you any right to test my damn blood? I didn't give y'all permission to touch me!" I was trying to think of anything to say to get out of the situation I had found myself in.

"You were hallucinating on the streets, and so you were brought in for treatment. Once you got here, we had to run tests so that we could properly treat you," she said, maintaining her professionalism.

"What do you mean I was hallucinating?" I was trying to

remember what the hell had happened that could have possibly led me to the hospital.

"You were convinced that you had had a conversation on a roof with a dead woman whose body was found weeks ago . . ." The nurse brought it back to me.

"No, you're mistaken. You see, I did have a conversation with a woman. And her name is Si-Si. She's my friend. And she's not dead. She was alive. She was talking to me. I was talking back to her and everything. I'm not crazy. I know what I saw."

"It's very common for a person with such high levels of cocaine in her system to hallucinate and see things that aren't there," she said, trying to convince me. "Now, you just lie down and get some rest. I will have a doctor come in and talk to you more about your condition, okay?"

"Yeah, please, do that. 'Cause you don't know what the fuck you talkin' 'bout," I said.

I was mad. I was on fire. The damn Dubai police done got me on this drug shit. I was about to have to do some serious jail time for partying. Hell, no! I needed to get the hell out of there. I just needed them to take them cuffs off me. That's all I needed so I could get up and haul ass out of that hospital.

"Celess?" asked a tall, light brown man as he entered the room.

"Bella," I said, surprisingly remembering that I was to use an alias.

"Well, yes, your ID says Bella, but we know who you are, Celess. Fingerprints have already been taken to confirm your identity. You're going to be extradited to the United States for charges of murder," the man said frankly.

"Who the fuck are you? You ain't no damn doctor!" I snapped at him.

"I'm a detective," he told me. "Your doctor will be in in a second."

"Well, that's the only motherfucka I wanna see and talk to!" I continued to snap.

Moments later the doctor appeared. "Hi, Celess, I'm Dr. Abdat," the short, dark-haired, dark-skinned woman introduced herself.

She sat down on my bed beside me. And right away she started rubbing my head as if to console me.

"You've had a rough time," she said. "Why not put it all behind you, now? Just turn all your troubles over to God. Surrender," she said.

At first I was frowning, ready to curse her ass out too. But she was so nice and warmhearted, I didn't feel the need to. I actually felt like I should listen to what she had to say. What she was suggesting was by far a better solution than anything I could think of at that moment. And it sounded so easy to do. Just turn my troubles over to God.

"Now you're going to go through detox here. Then once that's over, you will be transported from here to the jail—"

I started to object, but the doctor patted my leg. "Ah, ah, ah," she said, as if she was warning a baby not to do something. "Just listen, okay."

I held my tongue.

"You will be pardoned," she proceeded, "so that you can be extradited to the United States, your home. When you get there, you will be charged for whatever it is you allegedly did that led to your being on the run, and a bail will be set. You will then be given the opportunity to have a trial or to take a plea deal. After you make your decision and after you pay your debt to society, then you will be free of the demons you try to conceal with your drug use." She predicted my future.

I wanted to ask her how she knew so much about how the judicial process would be for me. I mean, she was a doctor not an attorney. Shouldn't she be talking to me about my treatment? I thought.

"I don't know you, Celess. But something tells me you've traveled this path before, which means God is trying to show you something. He's trying to teach you a lesson. And you're going to keep being thrown down this path until you get it—whatever it is. But the thing is, each time, the path is going to present more fear, greater danger, and while traveling it you're going to affect more lives. And until you learn the lesson God is trying to teach you, you will continue traveling this scary path, continue having bad luck, continue running into brick walls until your time is up," she said.

I remained silent as I listened to what the doctor was saying to me. It made sense. I couldn't deny that.

"Let me ask you something Celess," she said. "What was it that your friend was saying to you on the roof?"

I looked into the doctor's eyes, happy that she was giving me a chance to tell my side of the story, finally.

"She basically was telling me that she and I needed to part ways, you know, and trade in our destructive lives for something more fulfilling. She told me that that was what she had planned to do and whether I decided to do it as well was up to me, but she asked that I do." I summed up the conversation I had with Si-Si earlier.

"Hmm," the doctor said, a look of intrigue on her face. "Maybe you weren't hallucinating, Celess."

"Thank you!" I felt a strong sense of relief. "I knew it! It was real! That's what I've been trying to tell everybody this whole time!"

"Do you believe in spirits, Celess?" the doctor asked, seemingly overlooking my enthusiasm.

"What, like ghosts?"

"Ghosts, spirits, a presence from people who've passed on," she elaborated.

"I mean, I don't know. Why?"

"You should," she said softly as she rubbed my lower leg. "You should." Then she got up off the bed and headed toward the doorway of my room.

"Doctor," I called out to her.

She turned around.

"Why you say that?" I was curious.

"Because that's what I believe you saw on that rooftop today," she said simply.

Then a wave of clarity came over me, and I flashed back to when I saw Si-Si getting on the elevator. Thinking back, there was something very mystical about her—her being fully covered and then going to the roof without me. She didn't touch me at all. I didn't touch her. Then at the end of our talk she left the roof, walking in a totally different direction from the door.

A lump formed in my throat. Tears made their way down my face. Reality was setting in on me. The newspaper told the story accurately. Si-Si was gone.

The Aftermath

I was walking through LAX, my hands cuffed behind my back, my head lowered. There were cameras and press galore, taking me back to the days when I used to crave that kind of attention on various red carpets. But that day was a hell of a lot different. I wanted none of the spotlight then. I'd much rather have been a nobody that day than the Hollywood socialite turned murder suspect and fugitive that I was perceived to be by the entire world.

But what I wanted or didn't want was out of my control. My destiny had been sealed. And all I could do now was walk the path that was laid before me. I was facing twenty-odd charges, including accessory to murder, aiding and abetting, fleeing the law, possessing a false passport—the list went on.

I was jailed at the California Institution for Women in San Bernardino County while I awaited a preliminary hearing. Unlike what the doctor had told me back in Dubai, there was no bail set for me. I was a flight risk. I didn't mind, though. I was at a point in my life where I was just taking shit how it came.

It was a Saturday, a day when inmates could have visits. I

was asleep in my cell when an officer came to let me know that I had a visitor. I was shocked, as I didn't have anyone left in my life whom I thought cared about me enough to want to visit me in jail.

I was escorted to the visiting room. There were women at the various tables conversing, smiling, and laughing with their loved ones. I looked around for a familiar face, but I didn't see one. I was taken to a table where a white man was sitting. He was in a suit. Very formal for a weekend, I thought.

I sat down across from him, confused.

He held his hand out for me to shake, then introduced himself. "Celess, I'm David Pierre, one of the top criminal defense attorneys in the world. I've been hired to represent you by a mutual friend, Andrew Coselli."

"Andrew?" I smiled. "Wow, he's still alive?" I asked.

"Of course he's alive," the attorney said with a smirk on his baffled face. "Why would you ask that?"

I shook my head. "Just that he got to everybody else. I thought Andrew would be no different."

"Are you speaking of the man who murdered your and Andrew's friend, Sienna?"

I nodded. "Yeah, Chatman."

"Well, Andrew wanted me to tell you that he's been apprehended. Apparently an associate of his, goes by the name A.J., led police to him for the five-hundred-thousand-dollar reward money. He's back in jail, and the murders he's committed are going to send him to death row."

I sniffed, holding back tears of both joy and hatred for a man I had never met.

"As for you, I'm gonna help you win your case. I've reviewed your file, and I've had long talks with Andrew. Based on what I know so far, you were in a very rare position, where you had no choice but to do what you did." He was one of the few people who saw things my way.

"Well, I appreciate that," I told him. "I really do."

The attorney and I talked the entire visit about everything from my childhood to life in Hollywood to my drug abuse and even my most sacred secret. I revealed it all. I didn't withhold anything. And afterward, I felt so renewed.

Days had turned into weeks and weeks into months as my preliminary hearing approached. I was feeling pretty confident as I entered the courtroom knowing I had good representation. Then once inside the courtroom, I saw two people whom I'd least expect to see on my behalf—Michael and my mother. My heart skipped beats when I realized I had their support. I looked back at them and blew them both kisses. I was learning my lesson already, I could tell. And God was just as quick at showing me so.

My attorney and the D.A. congregated for some time before the D.A. agreed to drop all of the charges against me, with the exception, of course, of the fugitive and accessory charges, which, at the advice of my attorney, I pled not guilty to. A trial date was set for several months up the road.

During the time I was sitting, I did a lot of soul searching. I made every effort to get in touch with my spirituality. I read books, I wrote poetry, and prayed often—five times a day, to be exact. I had followed Si-Si's example, and I had taken my *shahada*. I welcomed Islam into my life and with that I welcomed truth, honesty, and complete submission to God.

My mom and I wrote to each other weekly. Come to find out, she was battling cancer and didn't want to die without reconciling with her only child. Had this been a year ago, I would have told her to go crawl up in a corner and die somewhere for what she had done to me. But I was a changed person. I had forgiven her and wanted nothing more than to be in her life for its remainder.

As for Michael, he visited me every chance he could. He let me know that while it was still difficult truly to come to terms with my true identity, he couldn't shake the strong feelings he had for me. And after a lot of pondering, he figured that he had grown to love me as a person, not as a man or a woman. And therefore, it was hard to dismiss how he felt about me. So he decided to stop trying to do so. He decided to embrace how he felt, and he came to grips with the fact that it was perfectly okay for him to love me for me.

My trial lasted four days. The jury deliberated for six hours. Based on the common human survival instinct of self-preservation around which my attorney built my case, they ruled in my favor, probably because, had they been in my shoes that day when that gun was pointed at my head, they figured they would have done the same thing I did. They too would have protected the person who saved their life.

A huge weight had been lifted off my chest as I heard the "not guilty" verdict read. I cried a river. I thanked God repeatedly for not ever giving up on me. Then as I was taken out of the courtroom, I looked over at Michael. He was holding up a small, open box. Inside it was a ring. I nodded at him, overwhelmed with happiness and a sense of peace.

Destiny fulfilled, I thought.

Acknowledgments

First and foremost, thank you, Allah! You've brought me so far and through so much. Everything I am, have, and dream is nonexistent without your will. I love you immensely.

To my husband, Rich, thanks for your strength and unmatched support. Without you my life would be so incomplete. You have my heart, my love, and companionship forever. We're almost there!

To my boys, Amir and Ace, you two give me breath. I live for you. Thanks for being the best sons a mother can have. I love you more than words can say.

To my family and friends, I value our closeness. I thank Allah every day for each and every one of you. I may not say it often, but I love you all and appreciate you greatly. You are my rock!

To my sisters and brothers, this has been a crazy time in most of your lives, and I want you to know that the most critical dictators of what your life will become are your choices. If you want life to get better, simply make better choices. I love you and wish the best for you even when you don't!

To Darnell, this is a special thank-you for holding Amir

and Ace down for Rich and me over the past year. You've been a blessing in our lives. Love you much, brother-in-law!

To Sulay Hernandez, Shida Carr, Martha Schwartz, and the rest of my Simon & Schuster family, thanks for your ongoing belief in me. I'm enjoying our journey and can't wait to see what the future holds!

To Liza Dawson and Associates, thanks for steering me in the right direction and for all the advice, words of wisdom, and explanations. I couldn't manage this business without all you do!

To my mentor and friend, Karen E. Quinones Miller, now more than ever I want to tell you I appreciate you. Like you said, God brought you into my life and me into yours for a reason. And I'm ever so grateful he did! Love you, sis, with all my heart!

To my fans and supporters, I want to take this time to tell you thank you sincerely. You are the reason I am where I am, and for that I couldn't be more thankful. I know times are hard right now and for you to still support my books despite this says a lot. All I can do in return is continue to work hard for you and give you exactly what you want and more!

To everybody else or anyone I may have forgotten, thank you, thank you, thank you!

Ya girl,

Miash

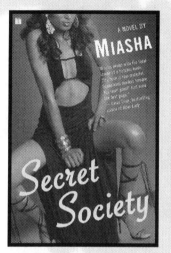

Printed in the United States
By Bookmasters